To Jeremiah

...He Is Able to do
exceeding abundantly above
all that we ask or think. Eph 3:20

CIRCUIT RIDER

H I Able

CROSSBOOKS
PUBLISHING

CrossBooks™
A Division of LifeWay
1663 Liberty Drive
Bloomington, IN 47403
www.crossbooks.com
Phone: 1-866-879-0502

First published by CrossBooks 02/21/2011

ISBN: 978-1-6150-7711-3 (sc)

Library of Congress Control Number: 2010943259

Printed in the United States of America

This book is printed on acid-free paper.

To my great-grandfather who was a circuit-riding preacher of the Gospel.

Acknowledgement

When I was twelve years old, an evangelist by the name of Merv Rosell came to our town to hold a ten-day evangelistic campaign. On the second Saturday of that campaign, he held a youth session, where he told a story that made an impression on my twelve year old mind, and which I have never forgotten. It is this story that I have taken the liberty of embellishing and using as the basis around which to build part of this book. Thank you, Mr. Rosell.

H I Able

Prologue

He squirmed uncomfortably as rain water dripping off the brim of his hat, somehow found its way inside his slicker and ran a rivulet down his back. The rain was now sheeting almost horizontally, and even though it was about three o'clock in the afternoon, it was as dark as night. Wind blew leaves and small twigs before it, which stung when they hit him. The air had a greenish gray cast to it, and he watched the sky anxiously for any sign of a twister.

"No fit weather for you or me, Noah," he spoke into the collar of his slicker. "I'm sure glad you are so sure-footed, or we'd be down in that gully for sure." The mule's ears flicked agreement, as he picked his way over the rocks of what passed as a trail. He was having a hard go of it, with the run-off turning the trail into a small stream.

"If I hadn't committed to being in Haskell tomorrow, I'd stop and make us a camp for sure. I may have to anyway."

Lightening was now flashing continuously, and the sound of thunder was constant above the roar of the rain. No funnel yet, but Preacher knew this was the kind of storm that spawned them.

The mule stopped in protest at what he was being asked to do. Preacher nudged his flanks with his heels, and urged him onward. After a minute, the mule complied, but Preacher knew that it wouldn't take much more for the beast to turn tail to the wind and rain, and no amount of urging would force him continue up the trail.

Animals are a whole lot smarter than we are, he thought to himself.

A blinding flash accompanied by a deafening roar cut his thoughts short, and he felt himself falling, then blackness…

BOOK 1

Chapter 1

It was the sun in his eyes that woke him and made him squint painfully.

Not yet! A couple more minutes, and I'll get up.

Morning sun! He came to his senses with a jerk. Something was wrong! This wasn't his bedroll. *Where am I?*

He forced his eyes open. At first he couldn't see anything but the glare of the low morning sun in his eyes. Morning! How could that be? Carefully he tried to move his hand. He found that he could, and felt something stick him. Then he smelled crushed pine needles.

Slowly, he turned his head and looked at pine boughs. *I'm in a pine tree* he thought. He tried to turn the other way to see what was on that side, but his head swam so that he had to lie back down to let the feeling pass. Instead, the feeling grew and his stomach heaved. *I must have taken a real wallop* he thought, lying back and closing his eyes.

He began to collect himself as he remembered the explosion. Yes, it had been an explosion. He saw again the flash and felt the blast that took him out of his old military saddle, the one given to him by that kind-hearted stableman whom he'd helped crawl out of a whisky bottle.

"Noah, Noah." he croaked. No sound. *Probably spooked and ran off. I hope he's all right*, he thought.

I'm not in a pine tree; I'm under a pine tree. Lightening must have knocked that fir right down on top of me. Wonder if anything's broke? The way his head hurt, it might be that. He felt the back of his head, and discovered an egg-sized knot, but no blood. *That's good.*

"Lord, this is a pickle! I don't know if I'm all in one piece or if I can get out from under this tree. You know that I am supposed to preach in Haskell Sunday morning, but if You don't help me, I'm not gonna make it. You know I always try to follow where You lead me, but this time, I'm really puzzled. I think I am doing Your will, so how did I get into this mess? Please help me, Lord. Amen."

He raised his arms above his head. Oh, his shoulders hurt, but they worked. He flexed his hands, wiggled his toes and feet, and raised his head again. They all worked, but something was holding him down, right across his thighs.

That could be bad ,he knew.

He raised his head and strained to see what was down there. One of the main branches of the tree was right in his lap and had him pinned securely.

He felt a moment of panic, as he realized that unless he could get himself out from under that branch, he very probably would die right there.

His panic gave him a rush of strength, and he grabbed hold of the branch heaving with all his might. Resting a second, he gave another heave. *No good!* He couldn't get any leverage to move the branch, and realized that even if he could get leverage, the tree was probably so heavy that he could never move it.

He lay back, as the momentary panic drained away and left him feeling exhausted. Worse yet, he was nauseated again.

"Lord, help me know what to do. I'm not afraid to come home to You, but I thought You had more for me to do. I guess that's my fleece, Lord. If You have more for me to do, then help me figure out how to get out of here. If not, I'll be like Paul. 'For me to live is Christ, and to die is gain'."

He began to look around at his circumstance and saw that the blow of the explosion had knocked him into a place where rushing water had eroded the softer ground along the trail's edge. He was lying in that erosion with the branch of the tree across him.

That's why I'm not worse hurt he thought. *If I can dig that erosion out some more, maybe I can slide out from under this branch.*

He began searching around for something to work with. The first things he found were some of the broken tree limbs, but they were too limber and blunt to be much good for what he needed to do, so he searched for something else. The rocks were too rounded and smooth to make good tools, and he couldn't break them.

He was about to give it up as impossible, when right at the limits of his reach he found a pointed rock. By straining he could barely scratch its surface with his fingers. Using one of the tree limbs he had discarded earlier, he tried to rake the rock to himself. But the limb bent too much to move it. Over and over he tried. He discarded the branch he was using and looked for another. Finally, he found another branch that appeared to be a little sturdier. He tried again. *No good!* Using the broken end of the branch, he poked at the soil around the rock, again and again. *I have to have that rock* he thought. *It's my only hope, except You Lord* he amended.

Did it move? It did! Not much, but it moved. Over and over he raked the branch across the rock he needed. He poked more around the rock with the branch, trying to loosen the soil. He broke some of the branches off the limb to leave short barbs that might hook the rock. *Yes, that might work.* Over and over, he tried. It moved again. *Can't quit* he thought, even though sweat was in his eyes and his vision was blurred. Slowly he moved the rock to where he could just reach it by straining as hard as he could. His fingers scrabbled over it then… he had it!

By then the mid-morning heat was making him sweat like he'd fallen in the creek, he was exhausted and his head was pounding. Thirst raged at him. The strain made him sick to his stomach, and he heaved until what little was still in his stomach was gone. The effort made him lightheaded, so he lay back again to collect himself.

He must have passed out, because everything went kind of gray and he couldn't think. When he came to himself again, he lay quietly regaining his strength.

After resting for a while, he went to work in earnest.

First he chipped at the ground around where he was pinned with the pointed rock. Then he pushed the dirt down toward his feet with the sticks he had. It was exhaustingly hard work that left him sick to his stomach, weak, and trembling, so he would stop, heave, and rest until he could continue.

Over and over he repeated the cycle, but still he was pinned. Sweat burned his eyes like fire, but he wouldn't quit. He worked the stick under his body and raked furiously.

"Lord, I can't believe You mean for me to die here without finishing what You called me to do. Please help me get free, so I can continue to preach Your Word."

Miraculously, he could move a few inches. With a cry of triumph, he renewed chipping at the wash-out. *Yes* he could feel that he was making progress!

Over and over he chipped and raked. Then, with a wrench and a rip of his pants, he slid free!

Chapter 2

Oh, it felt good to be out from under that tree! He was all scraped up and bleeding in a dozen places. He discovered that it hurt his hips bad to walk, but once he got going it was not unbearable. His shoulders hurt, too. He had blisters on his hands the size of eggs, which had broken and stung so much that it was hard to make a fist. He was dirty with mud and tree sap, and he smelled worse than … well, bad. Worse by far was his thirst! The constant strain, brutal work, retching, and sun had given him a raging thirst.

He made his way down into the bottom of the ravine and found rainwater in a small pool in some rocks. He brushed away the leaves floating on the surface, put his lips to the surface of the water, and tasted pure nectar. He drank slowly, so not to make himself sick again.

Which way did that mule go? he mused. *He wouldn't have gone far in that storm. Best thing to do is circle wider and wider 'til I run into him.* He set off as fast as his sore hips and pounding head would let him.

Shortly after noon, he found Noah standing in a deep patch of green grass. His head was down, not letting any of it get away. A small stream rippled through the little glen, so the grass was lush from the plentiful water supply. The mule's head came up when he smelled Preacher.

Preacher walked up to him. His bedroll and possible sack were still slung across the mule's withers. Preacher reached into the sack and got a piece of jerky. Sighing a long contented sigh, he chewed.

"Sure am glad to see you, Noah. Reckon I have some thanking to do before I do anything else." He put his head down across the old saddle, took a deep breath, and began to pray.

"Lord, I guess You know that I had my doubts back there. Guess my faith ain't as strong as I like to think it is, but You always come through for me. Even if I hadn't come out of that pickle, it would have been Your will, and that's all right with me. I don't know what You have in mind, but You brought me this far, and I'm trustin' You to see it through. Amen."

Here, he lifted his head, and was greeted by a sight that almost knocked him down.

Bursting out of the thicket surrounding the little clearing ran a woman… a girl, really. She had a bloody scratch across her face and an ugly bruise on her right shoulder. Her feet were torn and bleeding from running over the rough, rocky ground. Her hair was matted with leaves and pine needles. She was dirty as if she had fallen numerous times. Her eyes were wide and terrified and her face registered panic. Most notably, she was naked as the day her mother had brought her into this world!

She whirled in panic when she saw him, starting to run back the way she had come and then Preacher saw the welts across her legs, buttocks and back.

"Let me help, ma'am." he called.

She paused, unsure what to do.

"You're in trouble, ma'am. Let me help. I won't hurt you, I can help." He tried to keep his voice low and reassuring.

With that, he turned his back to her, slipped down his gallowses, and undid his homespun shirt. Taking it off, he handed it out behind himself without turning.

"Put this on until I can get something better."

Only a muffled sob.

"Ma'am, you sure do need help, and I'm offering to help you. I won't hurt you. Please put on the shirt." He still had his back to her.

Finally, trembling fingers reached out and took the shirt from his fingers.

"Thank you."

They were the first words she spoke, and were so soft and trembling he had trouble understanding what she said.

She jumped and gave a little cry. "They're coming," she sobbed, and now Preacher could indeed hear the sound of something big coming through the timber toward them.

"I'd rather die than let them catch me," she moaned.

Without a second thought, Preacher pointed up the hill. "There's a pile of rocks that way. I think I saw a small cave or den. You can hide there, and I'll try to throw them off."

She scrambled up the bank the way he indicated, and disappeared into the woods. He only had time to drop his head onto the saddle, and breathe a prayer. "Lord, I don't know what You're getting me into this time, but I need Your wisdom pretty bad."

He raised his head, and looked at four men on horses. One with a greener across his knees, and the other three holding six-shooters loosely pointed in his direction.

Chapter 3

"Well, what do we have here?"

He was a big man, close to six feet. He wore a wide-brimmed black felt hat, a white linen shirt, black broadcloth suit and string tie. He sat on the horse like he didn't much care for riding, and he was obviously the leader of the band.

"Who are you; and what are you doing here?"

"I'm a circuit-ridin' preacher on my way to minister in Haskell," Preacher replied. "Who are you?"

"I'm askin' the questions. What are you doin' here off the trail?"

"I had a little trouble with a tree back up the trail and my mule ran off. This is where I found him."

"How long have you been here?"

"Oh, about half an hour I would guess."

"This here is Brotherhood land, and you're trespassing," said the big man menacingly.

The other three men shifted in their saddles waiting for the big man to decide what to do next.

"I had no way of knowing that, it's not marked." Preacher replied.

The big man scowled at him. Preacher just waited.

"That can wait! We have more important things to be concerned with, now. One of our women got herself lost, and we're out to hunt for her. Have you seen anyone running through the woods?"

Is that why the guns? Preacher wanted to ask. Instead he said, "I caught a flash of something a while ago. But I couldn't tell what it was." Here he pointed back down the trail, where he had seen a deer bound away earlier.

The big man scowled some more and looked skeptical.

"Say, where is your shirt?" He pointed an accusing finger.

"I had worked up a good lather by the time I found my mule, so I took it off to cool down and put it in my possible sack. Here... I'll show you." Preacher moved to his saddle.

"Never mind! I'm Elder Eli Thomas, and you'd better be off Brotherhood land by the time we get back, or I may change my mind about you."

He wheeled his horse, and headed the way Preacher had indicated. The others followed, except for one, who sat scowling at Preacher in an imitation of his leader. Finally, after one last hard look, he followed the others.

Preacher took a deep breath thinking *that was fun, Lord.*

Preacher waited until he was sure the horsemen were out of sight. Then he took up Noah's reins and started up the bank toward the rocks.

Chapter 4

The girl was huddled in a tiny crevice, with Preacher's shirt tucked around her as best she could. She was shaking and crying. When she heard Preacher and Noah, she jumped to her feet, then into his arms.

She sobbed all of her terror and helplessness. She shook and sobbed until Preacher thought she would never stop. He just stood patiently without comment and let her cry it out. When the storm passed, Preacher got into his possible sack and retrieved the only other set of clothes he had... his Sunday preaching suit.

"These will have to do until we get into Haskell. It's all I have." he said, simply.

"I don't have any shoes, boots or moccasins small enough for you, but you can ride Noah so your feet will be all right."

She took the clothes, and went behind the rocks to dress.

When she came back, she asked, "Why are you doing this? This isn't your problem."

"That's where you are wrong." he countered. "It's my problem because the Lord sent me to meet with you." Her eyes grew big, and she looked frightened again, but didn't say anything more.

"We'd better get down the trail before those fellas come back and find us," he said. He gave her a leg-up onto Noah, took the reins, and headed toward the trail. They moved along for the better part of an hour with the only sounds being the birds singing, squirrels chattering, and her muffled sobbing.

Finally, Preacher said, "We've got a long way to go, and I'm a good listener. Maybe you would feel better telling me about how you came to be out in the woods in whatever trouble you're in."

Slowly, with many tears and long pauses, her story started to come out.

"My name is Elizabeth Strong. I'm sixteen… almost… well, in September." I'm an orphan, my parents died of the fever several years ago. The Brotherhood took me in and raised me. It's the only life I've known, since. It's a hard life. Oh, now I have nowhere to go and no one to turn to." She began to sob anew.

Preacher let her cry. When she had composed herself again, she picked up her story.

"You said that God sent you. Elder Thomas says he has God's ear. He speaks to us for God and tells us what God commands," she said solemnly. Preacher's eyebrows rose, at that.

She continued, "Elder Thomas is very strict. He is everything to the community; judge, jury, and executioner. His word is law. It was hard." she repeated, "but everything was tolerable until…." Her voice trailed off.

When she began again, the hair prickled on the back of Preacher's neck.

She cleared her throat, and picked up the narrative. "You see, E-Elder T-Thomas decided to make me his wife... his third w-wife, no fourth, he already has three."

Preacher looked back, and saw that her face was aflame with shame, embarrassment or confusion, he wasn't sure what. "What did his wives think of that?" He asked.

"Dame Thomas, his first wife, is a vicious, spiteful old woman who rules the household with an iron fist. The other two are afraid of her. She made it known that she would delight in showing me my place, and that Elder Thomas would soon tire of me once my p-prettiness f-faded." She was obviously very embarrassed by her revelation. She lowered her head, unable to continue.

"I couldn't stand it! The thought of being married to that horrid old man, and in the control of that viscous woman, made me sick. I was physically sick! So I decided there was nothing to do but run away."

"Where were you going to go?" He couldn't help himself. He was caught up in her story.

"I didn't know. Jeremy and ...." She stopped her eyes wide at the revelation. She continued in a small voice. "He was my...friend, my only friend in the community. Sometimes we would walk together by the creek, and talk about getting away from the Brotherhood. He said we could follow the creek until it flowed into a river. Jeremy said they build towns on rivers, and we would go until we found one. Anyway, it's what I tried," she said.

"Without supplies... or provisions?" Preacher was astounded.

"They caught me the second day."

The simple declaration brought tears to Preacher's eyes, which he quickly scrubbed away with a knuckle.

"What did they do?" he asked.

"They tied me up, and dragged me back to the community, and brought me in front of the council. Elder Thomas said I was a 'willful, rebellious and ungrateful girl who was to be sentenced to the circle for cleansing unto repentance'." She was crying too hard to continue.

Preacher let her cry. He knew this was a hard story for her tell, but the telling was like draining pus from a wound. She wouldn't begin to heal until it was done. They continued on without conversation for the next hour.

Chapter 5

When she resumed her tale, it was voluntary. It was as though she was ready, even anxious, to get it out. That didn't mean that it was any easier to relive...

"The men of the commune formed a circle on the public field. I w-w-was taken into the circle, m-my ropes were c-c-cut and m-my c-c-c-clothes were r-r-ripped off me." She was almost shouting now, trying to get it all out. "I was trying to cover myself from all those prying eyes. Then someone behind me stepped into the circle and struck me with his birch switch. They all had birch switches. Wherever I turned, someone behind me hit me with his birch switch. They were all screaming names at me, and the women stood outside the circle, throwing rocks at me as I was being tormented. Jeremy came running, he was screaming for them to stop. He said what they were doing was not right. He kept shouting that it was no way to treat a woman."

Good boy, Jeremy, Preacher thought!

"He said if they didn't stop, he was going to get the sheriff in Haskell, to make them stop. Then they all turned on him, and while they were arguing with him, I bolted."

"I ran as fast as I could. The women tried to stop me, but they are old, mostly fat, and slow. I had no trouble getting away from them. But the men were a different matter! They immediately gave chase, and some of them could run! When I got into the woods, it was better, but I thought I was caught more that once, especially, when they got on the horses to chase me. I ran and ran, and ran some more. I decided that I wouldn't let them take me back, and if they were going to get me, I would kill myself, somehow. Then, I thought I saw an angel."

Preacher was crying himself, now.

"He didn't chase me, or laugh and gawk at my nakedness, or try to hurt me. He spoke kindly to me; said he could help me; said he knew I was in trouble, and wanted to help me: I know he is an angel, because he told me God sent him."

When Preacher could find his voice again, he said, "I'm no angel, Elizabeth, I'm only a man who is a circuit-riding preacher of The Gospel of Our Lord Jesus Christ. Yes, I was sent by God to meet you in the woods, of that there is no doubt. I will tell you all about it. If I hadn't helped you when I had the chance, I would have been disobedient and someday I would have had to tell God why."

She frowned in confusion, "You said God sent you to me, but who is Our Lord Jesus Christ, and why do you preach His Gospel?"

"Ah, Elizabeth! If Elder Thomas did not tell you about Jesus, he doesn't really have the ear of God, as he claims. Let's take this slowly. First, I'll tell you why I know God sent me to meet you." With that, Preacher recounted his experience with the fir tree.

"So you see, God arranged for me to be in the precise spot at the precise time you would appear on the scene."

"Arranged? He almost killed you," she said heatedly.

"No, no, if He'd wanted that, I'd still be under that tree, and you'd still be running through the woods, trying to stay ahead of Elder Thomas and his tribe."

"Yes, I… I guess so" she stammered.

"Now you know why I believe God arranged for us to meet, and how He delayed my journey just long enough so that I would be in the right place when you came by," Preacher concluded.

"It seems so," she smiled.

"Now, something else is bothering me about what you told me earlier," Preacher said slowly.

"What is that?' Elizabeth frowned, trying to remember what she might have said.

"About Elder Thomas saying the he speaks for God. Yet he never talks about Jesus. I want to tell you why I don't believe he does speak for God, and may not even know who God is. What I'm going to show you will take some time. But we still have a way to go, so maybe I can get some of it done before we get into Haskell," said Preacher.

"What done?" she asked.

"Show you that Jesus is the only begotten Son of the Living God," he responded. "What do you know about the first people on earth?"

"Oh, you mean Adam and Eve?" Elizabeth asked.

"Very good, so you do know something about the Bible," said Preacher.

"Oh yes, Elder Thomas told us many stories, but he didn't mention any Jesus."

Well, you can't read the Bible without seeing Jesus all throughout. So, it sounds like he picked and chose what he wanted you-all to know about."

"What did he tell you about why Adam and Eve were thrown out of the Garden of Eden?" Preacher asked.

"They ate an apple they weren't supposed to," she said.

21

"Yes, the Bible just says it was fruit. We don't know for sure what kind it was, but the important thing was that Adam and Eve disobeyed God, and in so doing sin first entered man's experience. Do you know what they did next?"

"No," she said.

"They tried to fix it so God wouldn't know," he said.

"Oh yes, they sewed leaves together to cover their nakedness. I wish I had had some," she giggled.

Preacher laughed with her. It was a good sign that she could already laugh about it, he thought.

"Yes, but God wasn't fooled a bit. All it proved was that Adam and Eve knew they had done wrong. By that one wrong choice, sin entered the world and has been trouble for mankind ever since," Preacher said earnestly. "What did God do about it?"

"Uh, I don't know. Wait! Yes, He killed an animal and made them clothes."

"Right, again. This is the first time God stepped in to solve man's sin problem. He did it by shedding innocent blood, and this became the guiding principle to solve man's sin problems," Preacher explained.

With that, Preacher rummaged around in his possible sack and came out with a well-worn Bible, opened it, and as was said of Phillip in Acts chapter 8, he began to preach Jesus.

Chapter 6

"So, God knew that He would send Jesus into the world to fix our sin problem, once and for all, way back there in the Garden of Eden, when Adam and Eve were unable to fix it themselves, just hide it," Preached said. "Look there."

There was Haskell. The sun was sinking fast as they hurried onward.

Haskell wasn't much as towns went. The main street was a short block long. On one side was the sheriff's office with a single cell in what was barely more than a closet in the back. Next to it was the Mercantile, owned by hard-working Merton Lewis. Next to that was the only boarding house in town. Preacher knew it well. Widow O'Hanlan had a standing order for a room whenever he was in town.

The other side of the main street held the saloon, without which, it seemed, no town could survive. Incidentally, it was the only place large enough for Preacher to hold services in, so on Sunday mornings it was converted to a place of worship. Next to the saloon, was the livery stable, where Noah was bound for a well-deserved rest. At the end of the block, on the same side and separated by enough space for at least a couple more buildings, was a little one-room bank. It was owned by Judge Morris who wasn't really a judge, but everyone accorded him that title, out of respect, as the most important man in town.

Preacher led Noah down the street to the boarding house. He knew that every eye in town had seen them coming, so he wasted no time. He tied Noah's reins to the hitching post, helped Elizabeth down, and marched up to the door. Rapping smartly he called out, "Mrs. O'Hanlan, it's Preacher and I've brought a guest."

Elizabeth felt a little tense beside him.

He squeezed her arm. "Don't worry! Mrs. O'Hanlan will take you right under her wing," he whispered.

The door opened, and Mrs. O'Hanlan stood there eying Elizabeth suspiciously. She was a matronly woman of indeterminate age, with salt and pepper gray hair, and a kindly heart, as Preacher well knew. "Preacher, I expected you yesterday," she scolded. "Shure'n you look like you've been in a fight with a polecat… 'n lost"

"Mrs. O'Hanlan, this is Elizabeth, who will require a room as well," Preacher introduced as he guided Elizabeth into the parlor.

"Sure 'n ya' know that I wouldn't be considerin' such a thing if it wasn't you, Preacher." Mrs. O'Hanlan blustered. "This is a respectable boarding house, now 'tis."

"That's why I brought her here, to you, Mrs. O'Hanlan," Preacher said smoothly.

"Sure 'n has she got money? It'll be $1.25 per week, in advance. Breakfast and supper included," she said in her brogue.

"I'll pay her bill myself, Mrs. O'Hanlan. Her things haven't caught up yet," Preacher said.

"And why is she wearin' a man's clothes, now?"

"Do you remember the parable of the good Samaritan, Mrs. O'Hanlan? Elizabeth had a similar brush, and so I temporarily gave her my Sunday meeting clothes to travel in. As soon as I get her settled in, I'll go see Mr. Lewis about something more suitable," Preacher soothed.

"What? Why you poor dear, are you all right? Why, of course you'll stay here. I'll heat you a nice bath." She turned on Preacher, "You'll do no such thing. You won't be knowin' what a lady needs. I'll take care of her, myself. Lord, the ideas of you men! Bring in some more wood for the cook stove." This last was thrown over her shoulder, as she hurried Elizabeth up the stairs to an empty room.

Preacher chuckled. "Just as I expected, Lord, she needs someone to mother, and Elizabeth sure fills the bill."

Preacher walked outside, found the woodpile, and gathered an arm load. He walked back into the kitchen and deposited the wood in the wood box. Still chuckling, he went out to Noah and gathered his possible sack and bedroll, taking them up to his usual room. Then he went back outside to Noah, gathered the reins, and led him over to the livery stable. The livery man knew Noah and led him back to a stall. Preacher walked over the Mercantile. Mr. Lewis was still behind the counter.

"Hello Preacher, just get in?" he asked.

"Yep, how's business?"

"Good. You were sure right about carrying building supplies. They're building a new cabin west of here, and I've been selling them all of their building needs." As more people move in around here, it'll get even better," predicted the businessman.

"Great! Merton, I'm sending Mrs. O'Hanlan to pick up a few things for a lady I helped out along the trail. Could you put it on my account, and I'll settle up with you before I pull out?"

"Sure Preacher! I know you're good as your word."

"Another thing, Merton, she'll be around for a while, and will need a way to take care of herself. Any chance you could hire her to sweep up, stock shelves… things like that?"

"Well, I suppose so," he said thoughtfully. "But I couldn't give her more'n about two bits a day. If that would help, then sure."

"Thanks, Merton. I'll send her around. Make her think it's your idea," Preacher said.

"Sure thing."

"See you in church, Sunday. Say hello to the Missus."

Preacher then walked on down to the sheriff's office. "Hello sheriff," he called out as he entered.

Hello yourself, Preacher."

"So, how close is retirement now?" Preacher asked.

"'Bout this time next year, I guess. I got me a dep'ty that looks like he can take it over. I'm gonna move closer to my son, and do a little gardnin'."

"What do you know about Elder Eli Thomas, and a group he calls Brotherhood?"

"Not much! They're an unfriendly bunch; keepin' mostly to theirselves. Why? You run into 'em?"

Preacher outlined the story Elizabeth had told him. "They were a prickly bunch and if they're in the habit of treating womenfolk the way they did her, you may need to keep an eye on them."

Think they'll come in here after her?" asked the sheriff.

I don't think so, but you never know," said Preacher. "Merton is going to let her work around the store 'till she gets on her feet and decides what she wants to do. Mrs. O'Hanlan is busy motherin' her, so between them she is in good hands."

"Yep, best they is," agreed the sheriff.

"Just keep an eye peeled if you will, sheriff."

"Shore, that's my job."

"Thanks." Preacher called as he went through the door. It was about dark, so he headed for the boarding house, satisfied with the things he had set in motion.

"There you are," Mrs. O'Hanlan sniffed. "Chicken and dumplin's, tonight. Thought you were going to let it get cold! Hurry and wash up!"

Preacher knew from experience, better than to argue. He went to wash up.

Chapter 7

"She just up and disappeared, d*#@* it. Naked like she is, she won't last the week." Eli Thomas was mad, madder than they had ever seen him. He stomped around cursing freely. "How could you let a twig of a girl give you the slip, like that? She's got to be somewhere. She can't just disappear like smoke."

"Well, we rode pretty well all over outside the mouth of the canyon. We didn't see hide or hair of her nor any tracks, neither." retorted Toby, one of Thomas' lieutenants.

"I thought you had your eye on her in the circle. How did she get away from that? I… *we* had her right where we wanted her, and she slipped out. Grown men who should know how to handle a sprite like her, and you let her give you the slip"

"You were with us, boss. You know…"

"How many times do I have to tell you not to call me boss?" Someone's going to hear you and start asking questions." Thomas thrust his jaw in the face of the offender.

"I forget. Old habits are hard to break, an' you used to like it back in…"

"*Not* here, and *not* now, got it? I don't need these pilgrims gettin' spooky. I got 'em buffaloed and it's going to stay that way." Thomas' face was red and his eyes bulged in anger.

"All right, I'm sorry. I'll try to remember," said Toby sullenly.

"You'd better!" This last was more of a hiss, and the lieutenant dropped his eyes.

"Well, it's really Jeremy's fault. If he hadn't butted in like that…" offered a hard case known only as Jones.

"Yes, he has a lot to answer for. At the right time, I'll take care of him," responded Thomas. "Tomorrow, you take some men and ride down the creek," he said to Sam.

"She won't try that again. She knows we caught her there, last time," Sam objected.

Thomas whirled on the man. "I'm doin' the thinkin' and plannin' around here. You think you can take over?"

"No, no, I just thought…."

"You're not equipped to think, leave that to me. You just do what I tell you!"

"Yes, sir, boss …er …Brother Eli."

Thomas glared and then said, "She may be canny enough to think we might not expect her to try that again. That's why we'll check it out. She's got to be somewhere close. Her feet will be getting plenty sore."

"If you ask me, I think that preacher we found knows more than he let on. I didn't trust him then, and I don't now. I gave him the eye, pretty good, after you guys rode on. He looked nervous, to me."

"You may have something, there, Sam. Showin' up the way he done, at just that time and all…"

Thomas curbed his irritation. "Mebbe so, but I still got to think she went to ground. Holed up in some den or cave… some sort of shelter. She wouldn't go very far naked like she is. She's shy; she wouldn't want people to see her." He rubbed his jaw, thoughtfully. "But if he is helping her, there'll be h*** to pay. I'll settle his hash, but good. Nobody takes what's mine, and gets away with it, *nobody!*"

Chapter 8

Next morning, after a breakfast of scrambled eggs, ham, hot cakes, strawberries and coffee, Preacher felt fit enough to face the day, Brotherhood or no. He walked over to the livery stable to look in on Noah.

"He be fine." the stable man said with a chuckle. "He sounded off 'bout daybreak, fer his breakfast. Once he had that, it was out to the corral where he's been chasing that little molly ever since. She sure knows how to lead him a merry chase," he laughed.

"Elmer," Preacher said, "seen any new horses in town, since I got in?"

"Nope, just the same ones as usual," Elmer replied. "Expectin' somebody?"

"Could be! Ever hear of Elder Eli Thomas and the bunch he calls Brotherhood?"

"Oh, lawdy, yes! They's bad news, Preacher. Most unfriendly bunch I know."

"Well, I ran into them back up the trail, and they might be figuring on finishing our little skirmish. If you see them, or any of their horses, let me know. I'd just as soon they not sneak up on me unawares."

"Sure thing, Preacher. You got it."

Thanks Elmer," Preacher called as he left the livery.

Walking down to the saloon, he paused outside the batwing doors before entering. He always got that funny feeling, remembering how he used to push through these kinds of doors for other than holy business. That was back before the Lord got hold of him, and gave his life a new direction. As always, he breathed a prayer, "Thank You, Lord." He entered and paused to let his eyes adjust to the interior dimness. Mike was behind the bar, as usual.

"Hello Mike," said Preacher. "I just stopped by to make sure everything was all right for Sunday morning."

"Sure Preacher, as always. Territory law says I can't sell drinks from Saturday midnight until Sunday at sundown, so I can't use it. You might as well," said the bartender.

"Well, thanks, Mike," said Preacher. I would appreciate it if you could move the tables over into the corner and set the chairs facing that end of the room as usual," Preacher indicated with a wave. "We'll put it all back when we're finished."

Mike grunted his agreement.

"Will I see you in the service, Mike?" Preacher asked, already knowing the answer.

"Not me, Preacher. I'm too far gone there's no hope for me. God doesn't want anything to do with this guy." Mike looked genuinely embarrassed.

"You know better than that, Mike. It's never too late. The Bible says that God saves to the uttermost. If He could save me you're no problem for Him, whatsoever. We've had this conversation before. Remember the thief on the cross when Jesus died? He'll take you just like that if you will come to Him."

"Better give up on me, Preacher. I'm too far gone."

"I'll never give up on you, Mike. You're a good man. You just need Jesus."

"Thanks Preacher, maybe someday..."

"I'm praying for you Mike," said Preacher. No response. Preacher walked out of the saloon into the glare of the mid-morning sun.

When he got back to the boarding house, Preacher found that the women were back from their shopping trip to the Mercantile. Elizabeth looked like a new woman in a simple frock of blue and yellow flowered print, dainty slippers, and even a yellow parasol. She posed gaily for his approval, which he freely gave.

Mrs. O'Hanlan said, "Preacher, there's something else I want to show you."

She disappeared into the next room, and reappeared carrying an oilskin-wrapped package. "Didn't you tell me that you can play the banjo?" She held out the package. "This was my husband's, and I didn't think I could ever bear to part with it, but recently, the Lord's been working on me about it never being played, and well... I know you don't have one, so maybe this could help you in your preaching and ministering so... you take it." She thrust the package at him, and turned quickly away to hide the tears in her eyes.

Preacher opened the oilskin and slid out a banjo in perfect condition. It had obviously been lovingly cared for. Reverently, he strummed it. *Out of tune*, he thought.

"Wonder if it will still hold a tune?" He tuned it carefully, so as not to break a string not played in a long time. He strummed a few cords, then turning to Mrs. O'Hanlan, he gently kissed her cheek. "This is indeed a gift beyond compare," he said. It will be used for the Lord's glory and to do His work. I thank you with all my heart."

Then, what a fun time they had. Preacher played Turkey in the Straw for them *just to show them that he could indeed play*. They sang some hymns then Preacher slid the banjo back into its oilskin case. "I'll use it tomorrow in the service," he promised.

Mrs. O'Hanlan was obviously pleased at the reception her gift had been given, and she just beamed. Then Elizabeth told how Mr. Lewis, the merchant, had approached her with a job offer. "It will allow me to support myself, and pay you back for all you have given me," she said shyly.

"Pay back is not necessary," Preacher insisted. "But it's great that you can stand on your own, now."

"I have to put the finishing touches on my sermon for tomorrow, so I'll be in my room." He went up the stairs.

Chapter 9

Preacher stood outside the batwing doors of the saloon greeting people as they arrived for the service. It was still a saloon, still had the same bar, the same furnishings, even the same odor as it had had yesterday. But somehow it was different. God was being honored here.

It was about time to start the service. About 20 people had gathered in the finest they had. After all, this was the Lord's Day, and the only excuse they had for any kind of entertainment, much less worship, so nearly everyone from town was there. Even some of the farmers and ranchers had ridden in for the occasion.

Elizabeth and Mrs. O'Hanlan arrived and gave Preacher big smiles on their way inside.

Preacher walked up to the front of the room, picked up the banjo, turned and welcomed the people.

"Friends, it's good to see you all once again. It's been four months since I was last here, and I can see things seem to be going very well for you. Crops look good, business seems to be doing well, and everyone is healthy. In all, it appears that the Lord has blessed us all, and we have a lot to thank Him for this day. That's just what we're going to do. Stand up and greet your neighbors while I tune up this banjo. Then we'll sing some songs of thanksgiving."

There was a general shuffling as people rose and babble increased as they all began greeting one another. Preacher hit a few chords on the banjo, and the people joined in singing "We Gather Together to Ask the Lord's Blessing," followed by "Give Me That Old Time Religion" and "Amazing Grace."

Preacher offered the Morning Prayer, thanking the Lord for all His provisions and blessings. "Thank you in particular for the special gift of this banjo, to assist us in singing Your praises. We dedicate it to Your service, and ask Your blessings on the giver. In Jesus' name amen."

Mrs. O'Hanlan just beamed.

"This morning, the text for my message is found in Luke's gospel, chapter 19 the first 10 verses."

Preacher read the story of Jesus' encounter with the tax collector, Zacchaeus.

"In particular, I want to consider verse 10, where Jesus, referring to himself says, "the Son of Man is come to seek and to save that which was lost."

For the next thirty minutes, Preacher laid out the simple plan of salvation. Showing how we are all sinners without any hope of changing our own condition. How Jesus came to earth in God's perfect timing, to solve man's sin problem *once and for all*, as we're told in the book of Hebrews. How child-like faith in Jesus, as God's only begotten Son, will apply that solution in each individual's life. How God will extend His mercy to those whose faith is in Jesus' shed blood, because God doesn't see our sin any longer, but He sees Jesus' shed blood.

"In conclusion, we're told in scripture that, 'not by works of righteousness which we have done, but by His Grace He saved us'. We appropriate that grace by faith in Him. Please bow your heads. Is there anyone who has seen, perhaps for the first time, that the only way to restore fellowship with God that sin has broken, is to trust Jesus the Christ as your own personal Savior? If so, now is the time to do something about it. You can pray a simple prayer, right there in your seat. Just quietly say to Him, 'Lord Jesus, I know I'm a sinner, I can never make myself right with God. I know You came to earth to provide a way for me to satisfy God's justice and restore my fellowship with Him. I ask You to come into my heart and life. I thank You for Your willingness to make that sacrifice for me, and I trust You to make me Your child. Amen'."

"If you prayed that prayer and meant it, you are now a child of God. He adopts us as sons and daughters of God. The scriptures tell us that, 'Old things are passed away, behold all things are new'. If you prayed that prayer, please raise your hand to let me know. I'll pray for you in your new life and try to help you in any way I can."

Timidly a little hand went up, and Preacher breathed a little prayer of thanks as Elizabeth took her stand for Jesus.

After the service, Preacher stood by the batwing doors talking to the people as they left. There were lots of smiles and handshakes, some hugs from the women and one from a little girl.

"Why don't you just settle down here? We need you Parson," one woman said.

"He just hasn't shown me that I'm supposed to do something like that. Maybe some day He will," responded Preacher. "Until then, I'll get by as often as I can. Besides, I'm not gone again, yet. I'll be here for several weeks. I've heard rumors of someone planning a wedding. I'll have to take care of that before I can be on my way."

The people filed out, and it became a saloon again. Elizabeth took his arm as they began strolling along the board walk outside the saloon.

"I prayed that prayer," she confided.

"I know, I saw your hand. You know, Jesus said, 'He who confesses me before men, I'll confess before my Father in heaven'. It was important for you to raise your hand like that."

"I want everyone to know."

"I know, I remember that feeling," Preacher said. "But remember, it's not the feeling that's important. It's what God says that counts. John 1:12 says, 'But to as many as received Him, to them he gave the right to be called children of God'."

Just then, they heard moans, the sounds of heavy blows being struck, and men's angry voices. Preacher turned to look between the saloon and the livery stable. There, three men had a fourth man down on the ground kicking and beating him.

"Go get the sheriff," Preacher said to Elizabeth, as he turned up into the alleyway between the buildings.

Chapter 10

"You men stop." Preacher shouted, "can't you see, he's badly hurt?"

The men turned as one, and Preacher instantly recognized them as the searchers in the woods. Elder Thomas recognized him, as well.

"Well... you, again! Seems like you've got a nose for getting into everybody else's business. This is none of yours. It's a Brotherhood matter and we'll take care of it."

"You mean, you'll kill him," Preacher said.

"Like I said, it's a Brotherhood matter, so unless you want some of what he got, get out of here," Thomas menaced.

"And let you finish beating him to death? I don't think so," Preacher retorted.

"You need to be taught a lesson... take him boys."

The two brutes separated and began to advance on Preacher with clear intent in their eyes.

"Hold it right there." The command was accompanied by the sound of the cocking hammer of a six-shooter. "Nobody threatens the Parson in my town," the sheriff asserted.

The two brutes and their handler stopped short as they saw the star on the sheriff's vest.

"What's going on, here?" the sheriff asked.

"Nothing that has to concern you, sheriff. It's a Brotherhood discipline problem that we were taking care of until this busybody preacher horned in. It's none of your business," said Thomas.

"That so? I thought I was hired to make everything that goes on in this town, *my business*," the sheriff said softly.

"Well, you know what I mean. We're Brotherhood, we govern ourselves, have our own laws, and handle our own justice, that sort of thing. Didn't mean to offend you," Thomas said smoothly.

"Preacher, what is going on?" the sheriff asked.

"These three had the fourth one on the ground, beating him with whatever they could get their hands on, and kicking him," Preacher responded. "I don't know if he's alive or dead."

"Well, let's see," the sheriff said. "Here, help me turn him over."

There was a muffled gasp behind them. Elizabeth had followed the sheriff into the alleyway and was now staring wide-eyed in shock at the young man on the ground.

"Jeremy!" she breathed.

"My dear, I'm glad you're safe. You must have found someone to help you after all." Thomas glared balefully at Preacher. Menace seemed to surround him like a cloud.

Jeremy was obviously in bad shape. Not only did he not move, he had blood running out of his mouth, nose, and right ear. He also had a huge knot on his right temple.

"Looks like he could have one or two broken ribs too," the sheriff observed.

"He's barely breathing," Preacher said. "We've got to get him somewhere out of this sun."

"Bring him to my room. I will take care of him until... until..." Elizabeth burst out crying.

"I'll lock these three up until the circuit judge comes next month. He can decide what to do with them," the sheriff stated grimly.

"For what, sheriff? It was a fair fight, it may have gotten a little out of hand, but no crime has been committed. I tell you it was a Brotherhood matter," argued Thomas.

"I'm not so sure a crime has not been committed," answered the sheriff. "I'm going to let the circuit judge decide."

"Fights happen all the time and you don't lock up the participants," Thomas argued. He was growing agitated at the thought of being locked up in that tiny cell for a month.

"True enough," said the sheriff slowly. "But then, one of them isn't beaten to death, either. Let's go."

"He's not dead either. You just think he's in a bad way. Why, tomorrow he could be out on the street telling everyone he meets, 'you ought to see the other guy'."

"In that case, I'll apologize and let you go," answered the sheriff. "Now move."

"You can't just lock us up without a charge. Fighting is not a crime, what's the charge?" Thomas was losing the battle and was desperately looking for a way out.

"Well, I'm not sure," said the sheriff. "The circuit judge can decide the charge."

"Is there a city ordinance against fighting?"

"No." The sheriff pondered the dilemma. "All right, here's the deal. You go back to Brotherhood land, and stay there. If you or your people come into town, it will be only to conduct peaceable business. If you step out of line in any way in this town, I'll lock you up in a heartbeat. If this here boy dies, I'll be coming out there to arrest the three of you, and you *will* stay locked up until the circuit judge decides what to do with you."

Elder Thomas smiled. "Agreed!" he said. "Come on boys."

Everyone watched as they strode off, got on their horses, and started off. Thomas stopped and turned toward Preacher. "This ain't settled between us yet!" Then he spurred his horse after the other riders.

"Let's get this boy in out of the sun," said the sheriff.

Chapter 11

Mrs. O'Hanlan about went into shock when they brought Jeremy into the boarding house and took him up to Elizabeth's room.

"This is a respectable boarding house," she cried.

"Yes, it is," said Preacher. "That's why we're asking you to be like the Good Samaritan in the Bible, and take this poor boy in to nurse his wounds."

Somewhat mollified, she went to get clean sheets and towels and find something to use for bandages. Elizabeth seemed to have gotten over her initial shock and was busily trying to see to Jeremy's comfort.

"He's bad," said Preacher. Is there a doctor somewhere close? We need to know what to do for him."

"Doc Hanson does what he can, but he's more of a horse doctor, and the title is honorary," the sheriff said.

"Let's get him. Otherwise I'll have to ride to Cedar Gap to get the doctor there. That's a day's ride each way."

"I'll get Doc Hanson and be back in an hour or so," said the sheriff.

"Let's see if we can get his shirt off, so we can see if we can stop the bleeding, and see any other obvious injuries," said Preacher.

They rolled Jeremy to one side, then the other, taking off his shirt and long johns.

"Elizabeth, go outside while I get his pants off," Preacher directed.

"Nonsense," she responded. "He's dead weight and you need help. I've taken care of sick and hurt people before. Let's go." Preacher shrugged, surprised by her spunk. They set to work getting the rest of his clothes off.

"Dip one of those cloths into that bowl of cold water and put it on that lump on his head," Preacher instructed. "I don't know if it will help him or not, but it sure felt good to me when I had a knot on my head."

"He's got a gash on his head, too. It's bleeding pretty bad. Dip a cloth in the water and hold it over the gash, maybe that'll help stop the bleeding," Preacher suggested. He began daubing at the blood coming from the corner of Jeremy's mouth.

"Here, let me do that," Elizabeth insisted. "You say a prayer for him."

Preacher was embarrassed that he had not been the one to take the initiative and ask God for help and for wisdom in dealing with Jeremy's wounds. He had just been too busy doing, to think about praying. He thought about what he had heard about Martin Luther, the Christian reformer, who prayed two hours every morning, except when he had a particularly heavy day planned. Then he prayed four hours.

"Lord, we come to you right now because You are the Great Physician. You made us and know us better than we know ourselves. Jeremy has been hurt and we don't know what to do to help him, but You do. Please undertake for him in ways that we neither know nor understand. We ask You to spare his life but we would not interfere with Your great plan, so we will thank You no matter what. Please guide our hands as we attempt to help him. Thank You for Your answer. Amen."

They settled back to await the arrival of Doc Hanson.

Chapter 12

It was almost three hours before the sheriff, accompanied by Doc Hanson, arrived. The good doctor was bleary-eyed, having stayed up all night helping a mama give birth to her calf. Without a word, he marched into the room, over to the bed, and began to examine Jeremy. He hummed and clucked, poked and prodded. Finally, he looked up. "Why is it that you people never call for me, unless the patient is so far gone that you have no choice? What hit him, a mule?"

"Three men," Preacher answered.

"Well, they did a right good job... they did!" snapped the good doctor. "I can set the broken arm and splint it. I can wrap up the broken ribs and if they haven't punctured his lung, or if he doesn't get pneumonia, he'll probably recover. But the head is another matter. I can't do anything about the head. Cold cloths like you're doing, is best. If he recovers, he'll recover. If not, he'll die. I can't affect the outcome one way or another. Plenty of rest... but then it doesn't appear that he is going anywhere, soon."

True to his word, the good doctor set and splinted Jeremy's left arm. He took a sheet and tightly wrapped Jeremy's ribs. He took a needle and thread and stitched up the gash in his head.

"He must be turned over every two to four hours. If he gets pneumonia, he'll die, sure." With that, he left.

"We can take shifts," Preacher said. "You take the first shift and then I'll come in and stay the night," he told Elizabeth.

"No, he did this for me. It is my fault he's in this condition. I'll stay with him throughout," Elizabeth said.

"How do you figure it is your fault," Preacher asked?

"I'm sure that Jeremy came to town to do what he had threatened to do, to tell the sheriff what was going on in the Brotherhood. Elder Thomas and his bodyguards must have come after Jeremy and caught up to him in that alleyway. If it wasn't for me, Jeremy would never have defied the Brotherhood that way," Elizabeth said sadly. "Now, he may die because of me."

"You can't stay up all the time, you have to rest. You'll do him no good by wearing yourself out," Preacher insisted.

"There's room here on the couch for me to sleep. If he needs me in the night, I will awaken instantly. I did it when my mother was so sick, so I know I can do it. Please do not try to change my mind. I know what I have to do."

Preacher shook his head in wonder. She was making decisions far beyond her years.

For six days, Jeremy lay as a dead man. There was no response, his arms and legs were limp. It was as if he slept the sleep of death. Elizabeth would moisten his lips with a wet cloth, every hour. Then, in the early morning of the seventh day, Elizabeth heard something. She immediately sprang to Jeremy's bed side.

"Water," she heard, just a breath, but distinct. She grabbed a cup, filled it with trembling hands, and raised his head. She placed the cup to his lips. Water poured down his front, wetting the bedclothes. He choked and sputtered, but got some of the water down. She patiently held his head until he had had enough, and drifted off again. Then, she wiped up the spilled water as best she could, and lay back down.

The next four days were back to the same routine. It was as though he were dead with no response.

"Maybe I just dreamed it," she thought. "Maybe I just wanted it so bad, that I thought he woke up."

Then, the fifth morning when she awakened, he was lying there looking at her. She jumped to his bedside.

"Jeremy, oh Jeremy," she cried. "Are you thirsty?" He nodded.

She filled the cup, again. This time, when she lifted his head and put the cup to his lips, he drank without choking. When she took the cup away, he indicated that he wanted more. She filled the cup again.

"Are you hungry?" she asked.

"No," he whispered, and he closed his eyes and went to sleep.

It was a different kind of sleep, this time. He was restless and groaned from time to time.

Preacher thought that was a good sign because he was feeling pain. Dr Hanson sent some laudanum to help him with the pain, and it seemed to help calm him.

Mrs. O'Hanlan resigned herself to the fact that there were two unmarried adults living in one of her rooms. After all, it was apparent that nothing was going to happen with one of them unable to be out of bed, or care for his own basic needs. She made some broth, and Elizabeth patiently fed Jeremy with a spoon, bit by bit, as he could tolerate.

He still looked more dead that alive, with sunken eyes and gaunt paleness.

The gash on his head was now healed, so Elizabeth took out the thread. Other than that, he continued to progress very slowly. The first morning that he was able to get out of bed, with much assistance, and sit in a straight-backed chair, was a real victory. By the time they got him back into bed, he was even more pale, and sweating like he had run a mile in the heat of the day.

Having broken that barrier, Elizabeth and Preacher continued to insist that Jeremy sit up for short periods of time. At first, just once each day, as his strength grew, they increased it to morning and afternoon.

The worst symptoms Jeremy experienced were the headaches. They were incapacitating, causing dizziness, and blurring his vision. The only relief was provided by the laudanum.

"It may never get any better." said Doc Hanson. "We don't understand much about the head, and injuries to it."

"No, said Preacher, "but God does." They continued to pray for his complete recovery.

Chapter 13

As summer faded, and the leaves began to display the colors signaling their fall to the forest floor, Preacher became restless to get on with his ministry to other towns on his circuit.

Elizabeth's birthday was celebrated by Mrs. O'Hanlan baking a cake for her. Preacher bought her a yellow hair ribbon. Now she was truly sixteen years old.

"I was scheduled to be in Cedar Gap in early August, and September is about gone. You and Jeremy don't need me like you once did, so I think I should go see to things over there. Besides I've done everything needing to be done, here. I performed a wedding, christened a newborn, baptized you Elizabeth, and went through my whole store of sermons."

"Oh, Preacher, how can you say we don't need you?" Elizabeth wailed.

"Jeremy is able to be out of bed almost all the time, except when he has one of those blinding headaches," said Preacher patiently. "I can go to Cedar Gap and do my work. Then I'll check back later this fall or early winter, to see how you're doing. If you really need me, you can send for me in Cedar Gap, and I'll come back at once," Preacher reasoned.

"What about the Brotherhood?" Elizabeth looked genuinely frightened. "What will we do, if they try to come back to hurt Jeremy... or me?" she added in a small voice.

"The sheriff knows all about it, and is watching the Brotherhood. Besides, you have help that I can never give you."

"What?"

"God, Jesus, The Holy Spirit. Paul told the Philippians, "I can do all this through Christ Who strengthens me."

"Yes, I've learned that," said Elizabeth.

"I'm going to leave first thing tomorrow morning. Jeremy continues to improve each day, and you have work when you want it, at the Mercantile," Preacher summed up. "Just be careful, and let the sheriff know if any of the Brotherhood shows up."

"Thank you Preacher, for everything." She had tears in her eyes.

"What's this?" Preacher asked. "I'll see you again in a few weeks if that's the Lord's will."

"But I'll still miss you," she said.

Preacher smiled at her and went to get his things together. Before daylight, he was on the trail.

Chapter 14

Preacher threw himself into the work in Cedar Gap. The town was a little larger than Haskell, and the people had gotten together since he had been there last, to make plans for a small country church. They had the foundation set, and some walls framed, by the time he rode into town. With eager anticipation, Preacher joined into the flurry of planning and building. Construction would be of pine logs, and a pile of cut, peeled, and notched logs was growing by the day.

The weather was holding in Indian summer beauty, so Preacher reasoned that the people would be encouraged by holding services on the church site, even though the building was not close to being completed. Accordingly, he announced that Sunday service would be at the church site with people sitting on the ground or chairs they brought with them. Women would bring food to share with others, and there would be a time of fellowship after the service.

The day dawned bright and clear, and people began arriving early. Horses and wagons or buggies were hitched away from the meeting site. Everyone was excited, and there were many smiles and friendly greetings. Preacher was everywhere, smiling and shaking hands. By the time everyone had arrived, there were thirty to forty people. Finally, the people began to sit down for the service to start.

Preacher got up, strummed his banjo, and began to sing the Doxology. The people joined in; then Preacher said a prayer.

"Lord, evidence of your blessings on this group of your people, stands here before us. This house of worship is an important reminder that You are with us each and every day, and our hope is in You. Help us to finish the task we have started, and say to the surrounding world that you are the center of this community. Amen."

They sang some more hymns; then Preacher took up his Bible for the morning sermon. Someone pulled a wagon over, and Preacher climbed up into the back of the wagon, so people in the back could see him better.

"My text this morning is from Ezra 3:7-13, an account of Ezra supervising the rebuilding of the temple." Here, he read the scriptural account of the great joy of the people, and the celebration at the completion of the building.

"We're standing today at the site of our house of worship. It is progressing, but with winter coming on fast, we may not get it done before snow flies. That means that we won't be able to hold meetings in it until next spring."

"No!" came the cry. "We want to complete it now."

"Can we do it before snow flies?" Preacher shouted.

"Yes!"

Preacher went on with his sermon, and the people became more and more committed to completing what had been started.

"There will be hardships, setbacks, opposition. Ezra had them, we will, too," Preacher cautioned. "But if God is in this, we can do it."

"Yes, yes!"

"Who will help us get the job done?" Preacher asked.

A dozen men stepped forward.

"All right, we start on Monday morning," Preacher stated.

The women broke out the food, the men stood around planning what they would do come Monday morning, and the children began playing tag.

Soon the cry of, "come and get it" was heard. So everyone stopped what they were doing to gather around the tailgates of wagons that had been set up as tables. They were loaded down with cold chicken, salads of every description, homemade bread, jams, preserves pies and cakes. Preacher asked God's blessing on their fellowship and the food, and then everyone set to with a will.

"Good sermon, Preacher."

"Gave us new vision."

"I'll lay you a plank floor, so smooth; you won't know it's rough hewn!"

And so it went. When people began to drift away toward home, there was still an excited anticipation.

Preacher smiled to himself, pleased with the way God had blessed his efforts.

Chapter 15

On Monday, true to their word, the men showed up early with hammers, saws, and axes to go to work. And work they did. What had taken a week to accomplish was now completed in a day. Soon the walls were up and the roof was being started.

Preacher was everywhere, encouraging, hammering, helping. He was on the roof that afternoon, nailing down cedar shingles which were being hand-split as they were being used, when suddenly, he couldn't move. He thought one or some of the men were playing a joke on him, so he turned to confront the prankster, but no one was there! *What's going on*? he thought.

Finally, he looked down, and found that the tail of his shirt was nailed into the new roof!

"Would you look at that." he said to one of the men working with him.

"Looks like we'll have to tear that section out and redo it," said the man.

"No we won't," said Preacher. "You got a jack knife?"

"Shore do," the man responded.

"Then cut 'er off and let's keep going," Preacher instructed.

The man laughed, "Now, this really is your church, Preacher."

"No. It's Gods church, He just needed my shirt tail to make sure it holds together."

The men got a good laugh out of the story, as it went around, and Preacher was ribbed good-naturedly all afternoon.

When the men quit to go home that afternoon, the exterior of the little church was complete. Tomorrow, they would begin putting in the plank floor, and doing finishing work.

"We'll build benches, and hold service in here on Sunday morning," Preacher announced. "Good job, men."

Next morning, most of the men returned. A few had to take care of ranch chores, delayed by their participation.

Work still went on at a good pace. Over the next few days, the building was finished. Gaps between the logs were chinked and the plank floor laid. It was indeed a thing of beauty that most homes still did not have. Shutters were made for the windows, which would be open in the nice weather. A sturdy door was built and hung on hinges supplied by the local blacksmith. The interior logs were whitewashed. Benches were made to accommodate thirty people. More would be added as needed.

Last, a privy was built. "Got to provide for human needs, the men said. "We can just go off in the trees, but the womenfolk need some consideration," was the reasoning.

On Sunday, the building was finished enough for use, and buggies and wagons pulled up early to enjoy the sight before the service started. A little steeple had even been added to denote it as a church, though no bell was available to hang in it.

Preacher stood outside the door, greeting people as they arrived.

When the service started, Preacher said, "You folks are the first ones to attend Sunday service in our new church building. It is due to the diligent help many of you men have given, that made this day possible. Praise the Lord, there were no injuries in the construction process."

"Except to your shirt," called a voice from the back. Everyone laughed at that.

"Yes, and that shirt has been retired. It will hang in memorial in the entrance," Preacher laughed.

Everyone clapped their approval.

"Now, it is only fitting that we dedicate this church as a community meeting house, and a Sunday meeting house, as well. Accordingly, I have asked His Honor the Mayor to say a few words. Mr. Mayor…"

Mr. Green, the Mayor, obviously pleased to have an official part in the dedication, rose to his feet, cleared his throat, and said, "My congratulations to you all on a job well done. This building is a tribute to what we can accomplish when we work together to a common end. I am delighted to have a hall to hold community meetings, and hope that Sunday services will be a regular event." With that, he sat down.

Everyone applauded; surprised that he hadn't used the occasion to campaign just a bit.

"Thank you, Mayor." said Preacher. Now, Mr. Mason from the Mercantile has asked to address us. Mr. Mason…"

"Thank you, Preacher. On behalf of the merchants in town, I would like to welcome this church to the community. We consider it a sign of stability and progress in this town. The Mercantile would like to donate six brass kerosene lamps to the church, for lighting."

A cheer went up, and an excited buzz rose.

Preacher stood back up. "Thank you, Mr. Mason for your generous donation. Now let us officially dedicate our new building to the Lord's work. Please stand with me and bow your heads."

"Almighty God, maker of all things in heaven and earth, sustainer of life, and giver of every good and perfect gift, we come before you this day with full hearts for your hand of blessing; for the beauty of the day you have given us; for the satisfaction of seeing the fruit of our labors, for these people who have given freely and sacrificially to bring us to this point. We know that Your church is not this building, but the hearts of all people who have placed their faith in Your great sacrifice on our behalf. This is a mere building made with our hands; a symbol for the world to see and be drawn to. It is but a tool that we dedicate to the spread of your gospel in this place. Now, be pleased to bless it and us to Your service. In the name of Jesus, our Lord, Amen."

"Amen," the people echoed.

Chapter 16

The days flew by. Harvest parties gave way to Thanksgiving. Preacher preached the funeral of one of the original ranchers in the area, John Davidson.

Even though the church members were lobbying hard for him to stay on and become the permanent pastor, Preacher knew he had other work to do, in other towns, so one day after Thanksgiving, Preacher announced that he would be moving on. There were some tears and passionate arguments for him to stay, but the day came when Preacher climbed aboard Noah, on that old military saddle, slung his possible sack, bedroll, and banjo across Noah's withers, and headed back to Haskell to see how things were progressing there.

As he rode into town, he met the sheriff.

"Howdy, Preacher," said the sheriff. "We're gonna have snow, any day."

"Probably, how're things going? Any more trouble out of the Brotherhood?" Preacher asked.

"Nothin'! They ride into town, do what they have to do, and skedaddle back to they own place."

"That must make everyone happy, I suppose," said Preacher.

"Yep, it shore do."

"How's Jeremy doing?"

"Fine! You'll see for yourself, soon," Sheriff shook his head. "Youth, it's a wonderful thing!"

"See you later, Sheriff."

"Shore thing, Preacher."

Preacher rode on to the boarding house. Mrs. O'Hanlan was out sweeping her porch.

"So you're back, Preacher," she called. "Room's just like ya left it."

"Thank you, Mrs. O'Hanlan. The banjo is sure a big help in my meetings," he added.

"I knew it would be." She smiled.

Preacher hitched Noah, and took his possible sack, bedroll, and banjo up to his room. He was going back to take Noah to the livery when he was almost run over by Jeremy.

"Preacher! It sure is great to see you back. I've been waiting for you to get here."

Jeremy, you look great! How're you feeling?" Preacher asked.

"Pretty good most of the time. I still get headaches, and they can be pretty bad. My vision gets blurry, and I get too dizzy to stand. But it's getting better every day."

"Well, you look good, your color is good, and it looks like you're moving pretty good."

"Yes, I'm doing good. The fact I'm doing so good is because of Elizabeth. I couldn't ask for a better nurse. That's why I've been waiting for you to get back. I love her, Preacher, and I want you to marry us," he blurted out.

"Well now, that's fine, it surely is. What does she think of it?" Preacher asked.

"Oh, I know she loves me, too but I've been waiting for your return to ask her. I want to surprise her. Come on, let's find her!"

"Hold on, there are a couple of things we have to clear up, first. You know Elizabeth is a Christian. She gave her heart to Jesus, and His word tells us Christians not to be bound together to unbelievers. Before I can marry you two, I need to be certain of your spiritual condition."

"Yes, Elizabeth talked to me about my spiritual condition. She told me all about Jesus, and the sacrifice He made for my sin, on the cross. She told me all about the prayer she prayed to ask Jesus to be her Savior."

"She did? That's great! What did you think about all that?" Preacher asked.

"It's great! It sure has made a difference in her life," Jeremy responded.

"Maybe it's time you did the same, and asked Jesus to be your Savior," Preacher said hopefully.

"I don't have to," Jeremy replied.

"It's not something one person can do for another, Jeremy. We all have to make the decision to follow Jesus individually. Why don't you think you have to?" Preacher asked.

"Because you only have to do it once, and I already have," Jeremy grinned.

"That's great," Preacher enthused, "with Elizabeth?"

"Yes, she helped me with the prayer."

"Why that little missionary," Preacher grinned. "Of course, it will be my joy to marry the two of you. Still it worries me just a mite to have you two here where the Brotherhood can make trouble, but God will take care of you."

"Well, if we can get to Ohio, I have an Uncle who has promised to teach me his business. That may answer your

65

concern," Jeremy said earnestly. "But first things, first, let's go find Elizabeth. I can't wait!"

He grabbed Preacher's arm and headed for the Mercantile.

He burst through the door. "Look who I found!" he shouted.

"Preacher!" Elizabeth exclaimed, and ran over to give him a hug.

They exchanged news for the next ten minutes and then Jeremy said, "Elizabeth, I have something I need to ask you."

"What?" she asked, all unsuspecting.

Jeremy dropped to one knee and took her hand. "Elizabeth, will you do me the honor of becoming my wife? Will you marry me?"

What happened next, just about floored Preacher.

"No."

Chapter 17

"No, I will not marry you," she repeated. You know I love you, Jeremy, but I can't marry you." She turned away, her face a sea of emotion.

Jeremy got slowly to his feet, his face a mass of disappointed confusion. "You love me, but you can't marry me? Elizabeth, dearest, that doesn't make sense! That's what people do when they love each other. I've just been waiting for Preacher to get back here, so he can marry us. I've been waiting so long!"

Preacher had to smile at that. "Maybe I'd better let you two kids talk this out. I'll be at the boarding house."

"No!" they both shouted in unison. "You're the reason I can't marry him," Elizabeth blurted out.

"Now hold on!" Preacher said. "How is it my doing that you won't marry Jeremy?"

Elizabeth turned away, her face aflame. "I-I didn't say it was your doing," she stammered.

"Then what did you mean," Preacher persisted?

"I-I can't say," she was becoming more agitated. Tears started to well in her eyes.

"I think you'd better explain, Elizabeth," said Preacher. "What you're implying is pretty serious, and I believe that I've always acted in your best interest, and been a perfect gentleman with you."

"Oh, you have, you have," she cried.

"Then please explain, and that is not just a request," he said.

"I can't, I just can't," she wailed.

"Come on Jeremy, said Preacher. "We'd better let her alone so she can compose herself." They walked back to the boarding house, neither of them feeling very talkative.

A few minutes later, Elizabeth came in. "Mr. Lewis sent me home until I feel better," she explained. I-I've been thinking all the way that I know I have been unfair to both of you. You deserve an explanation. S-s-so here goes. I don't want to say this, a lady does not just throw herself at a man, but you're forcing me so… Jeremy, I told you how Preacher rescued me when I was running in the woods. He saved me from who knows what Elder Thomas and his men would have done to me. I owe him my life, and so much more. He taught me about Jesus, and what God is really like."

"Yes, you've told me all that," said Jeremy.

"What I haven't told you is that he has told me how long and lonely the trails are. How often he talks to Noah, just to hear the sound of his own voice. How he's out in the wind and rain, and we know about the lightening. I love you, Jeremy, but I love Preacher, too, and… I've decided to take care of him from now on, if he will have me." Her lovely face was crimson, but her eyes were defiant as she finished.

Preacher's mind was in turmoil! He couldn't think straight. The room began to spin, and he had to sit down. He thought about all Elizabeth had said. Yes, the nights were lonely, the trails were long. Snow, sleet, wind, rain and sun were only the physical discomforts. There were the times he longed to have someone with whom to share victories as well as defeats. And he was tempted. *Lord, You know how I'm tempted to accept the offer being made by this lovely young girl,* he thought. *I've been alone for so long.*

He cleared this throat, wanting to be very careful with his reply.

"Elizabeth, what you have just given me is the greatest gift I've ever received, apart from my salvation. I'm humbled to think a beautiful young woman, like you, would think so much of me. I love you, too. But not like a man loves his wife. It's more the love and sense of accomplishment and pride a man feels for his daughter. I'm proud to have been able to contribute to your life. You've given me far more that I have ever given you."

"Any man would be proud and honored to have you as his wife, to stand beside him throughout all of life. I know I would be. But it just wouldn't work for me, for a lot of reasons. Let me tell you some of them. First, I've already told you that I don't love you the way a man loves his wife. That's not to say I couldn't or wouldn't, but that's where I am right now."

"Next, I am almost three times your age. Ah, ah before you open your mouth to protest, consider that it may not matter to you now, but as we grow older, it may become more and more of an issue to you. You need someone younger. Someone you can have a family with, can build memories with, and can grow old together with."

"God has called me to a work that takes me away for long periods of time. Not a good situation for a family. He hasn't told me to do anything different, so I'm going to continue until He shows me differently. I can't do otherwise."

Preacher paused to collect his thoughts before continuing.

"Preacher, I've thought of some of that. But I'm young and strong. I can go with you on the trail. I can be there to listen to you, and comfort you when things go bad," argued Elizabeth.

"You still have not addressed the main issue," said Preacher.

"What is that," asked Elizabeth?

"You love Jeremy.

"I love you, too"

"Not the same way you love Jeremy though, do you," Preacher persisted.

"Well, no but..."

"You need to be true to your heart, Elizabeth." Preacher interrupted. "If you married me, feeling as you do for Jeremy, it would be a sin."

"Well, wouldn't it be a sin for me to marry Jeremy, feeling as I do about you?" Elizabeth reasoned.

"No, I don't believe so, and here's why," Preacher countered. "I believe what you feel for me is gratitude and a sense of obligation, not romantic love. You still have not accepted the fact that you don't owe me anything."

"But you saved me from..."

"God saved you." Preacher interrupted, "both your physical body, and your soul. I was just His tool to do so. If I had been disobedient, He would have used some other way to accomplish what He was going to do, and someday I would have had to tell Him why I didn't do what He asked me to do."

"Oh, I don't know, I'm so confused," Elizabeth moaned.

"I know you are, Elizabeth. Just think about what I have said. We can talk again, later."

Preacher stood up. "I'm going over to check on Noah," and he left, glad to be out of that emotionally charged atmosphere.

That night, Elizabeth didn't show up for dinner. Preacher, Jeremy and Mrs. O'Hanlan didn't have a lot to say, so dinner was rather quiet. After dinner, they all just turned in.

Chapter 18

Next morning, when Elizabeth came down for breakfast, it was evident that she had slept very little, if at all. She tried to smile, but her heart wasn't in it.

"Good morning, Elizabeth," Jeremy said. He didn't look any better.

Preacher's eyes were gritty from lack of sleep, and he had a headache. *Poor Jeremy*, Preacher thought. *If his headaches are worse than this, he must have real trouble even getting out of bed.*

Only Mrs. O'Hanlan seemed to be in good spirits. "Faith 'n b'garra,." she said, "love is supposed to make you happy and carefree, not grumpy." It didn't seem to help.

After breakfast, Elizabeth went off to the Mercantile, and Jeremy went for a long walk, which left Preacher on his own.

Preacher sat down with his Bible and began to meditate and pray. "Lord, I think I'm doing the right thing. All the things I said to Elizabeth yesterday are true, but I don't want to hurt her or ignore You if You are opening a door for me, that I'm too blind to see. She is a lovely woman, and You know I have been lonely. Show me, what is Your will. If I am supposed to take her to wife, give me peace about it and Jeremy grace to accept it. If not, give me peace to say no and Elizabeth to understand. Either way, they are great young people, Lord, with many years ahead of them to serve You. May they be faithful and obedient to wherever You lead them. Amen."

The more he read and meditated, the more Preacher's heart became peaceful about his decision.

That evening, when Elizabeth came back to the boarding house, she seemed more at ease, more settled. "Where's Jeremy?" she asked Preacher.

"He's out, and I would expect him to come back any time," Preacher responded.

Sure enough, a few minutes later, Jeremy came in.

"Sit down, both of you," Elizabeth directed. "I've come to a decision, and we need to get this settled."

I've wrestled with this all night, and all day," Elizabeth began. "I've reached a decision, as I said. Preacher, I love you very much. You are kind, generous, fun to be around, and you're always there when I need you. In fact, you remind me of what I can remember about my father. I will always love you… as I do my father."

"Jeremy, when I think about you, my heart just stops. When I think about not being with you ever again, if I marry Preacher, I can't breathe. I love you so much that it hurts when we're apart. When I think about it, I have to marry you, Jeremy… if you still want me," she said in a tiny scared voice.

"Still want you? You silly goose, if I didn't still want you, I wouldn't have been about to go crazy all day!" He began dancing her around the parlor.

She stopped him when she got too dizzy to stand. "Preacher, I still want you… to give me away. As an orphan, I don't have a daddy to do it, and I can't think of anyone I would rather have do it than you."

"Child, it will be my pleasure and honor, to do it," Preacher said solemnly.

"This is just perfect," Elizabeth bubbled. "I just wish I had my mother's wedding dress. She saved it for me, and I was always going to wear it when I got married. But that's not what is important. We're getting married! I love you, Jeremy!"

"Well, where is this dress, now?" Preacher asked.

"It is in my trunk, back at the Brotherhood village. I'll just have to do without it."

Preacher and Jeremy exchanged a look.

"When do you want to do this?" Preacher asked.

"The sooner, the better," they both said in unison.

"Well, I think it would be good to announce it to the community, and give them a chance to get used to the idea, don't you?"

"I guess so," Jeremy conceded.

"This is November 29th, what about two weeks?" Preacher suggested.

"That would be all right, it would give me time to get ready," Elizabeth blushed.

"All right, December 13th, no the 14th."

"Ya ain't getting' married in no saloon, neither," Mrs. O'Hanlan chimed in. "It'll be crowded if we have to have it in here, in the parlor. But we should be able to have it outside, in the garden."

"If not, the parlor it is," agreed Elizabeth.

Preacher's eye met Jeremy, again. He gave a little nod, and Jeremy nodded back.

The excited buzz of wedding planning rose higher as Jeremy and Preacher slipped out the door.

"Are you thinking what I'm thinking?" Jeremy asked.

"Probably," preacher conceded. "Let's go see the sheriff."

Chapter 19

"Why shore, a purty girl like that should have her weddin' dress!" The sheriff emphasized his point by slapping the desk top. "After what those galoots pulled on you," here he looked at Jeremy, "they better not give us no trouble about it neither. It's too late today, but tomorrow you be in my office bright and early. We'll have that trunk before nightfall."

"Thanks Sheriff, we'll be here," Preacher promised.

Next morning, Preacher and Jeremy, on a pair of rental horses from the livery, and leading Noah outfitted with a pack saddle, showed up at the sheriff's office. The sheriff and his deputy were all set to go. Sheriff pulled a saddle gun out of the cupboard and tossed it to the deputy, taking one himself. "Just in case," he said. He jacked a shell into the chamber, set the safety, and slid it into the saddle scabbard. "Guess we're ready," he said. "Let's go."

Off they went at a fast pace, and by noon, they were on Brotherhood land.

"Their town is through that gap and up that canyon," Sheriff said. "Go easy, now. They may already know we're here." He led the way up the draw.

"Halt!" a voice called. "You're on Brotherhood land, and you're trespassing."

"It's Sheriff Micah Tate out of Haskell. I'm here on official business."

"Hold on." A messenger was obviously being sent, and word of what to do was awaited.

A few minutes later, the messenger got back. "You have no jurisdiction here. Leave."

"No," said the sheriff, "but the federal marshal coming next week, does have jurisdiction. Would you rather take it up with him?"

Preacher looked surprised. "I didn't hear about the federal marshal coming," he said.

"He's not, but they don't know that," the sheriff said in a low voice.

"Wait a minute!" came the command.

After several minutes the voice said, "All right, drop your weapons, and you can advance."

"No deal." the sheriff countered. "I'm the law, here. Either we come in peaceful like, and do our business with Elder Thomas, or you take the consequences. Your choice!"

More waiting.

"All right, come ahead."

A band of men materialized around them, and their horses were led into the compound.

Curious eyes watched as they were led to the largest building of them all. There Elder Thomas himself awaited their arrival.

"What do you want here? The whelp is obviously recovered, so you're not here for that."

"We are here to retrieve the trunk belonging to Elizabeth Strong."

"We have only Brotherhood property, here," snapped Thomas.

"It belonged to her parents, and contains all she has left of their memories," the sheriff continued patiently. "She says it is here, and we are prepared to search house by house until we find it," said the sheriff unflinchingly.

Thomas glared at the party. "You wouldn't dare!" he hissed.

"Willing to bet the pot on that," the sheriff shot back.

The battle of wills continued, with Elder Thomas flinching first. He gave a little wave of his hand, and some men went scurrying. Within a few minutes, they returned, carrying a trunk between them. They set it in the dirt in front of Elder Thomas.

"There's what you came for, now get out! Get off Brotherhood land before you feel our wrath!" Thomas blustered.

Preacher and the deputy dismounted, and got the trunk, hoisting it up on the pack saddle and lashing it into place.

"And you," Thomas glared anew at Preacher, "Preacher, or whatever you call yourself, we're not finished yet! Not by a long shot!"

Preacher turned slowly to Elder Thomas. "Bring it on, Thomas. My God has brought me through a lot of things, and He will have no trouble handling the likes of you."

The party turned and started back through the canyon.

Sheriff said, "Me first, then you, Jeremy, then Preacher and last the deputy." And keep that saddle gun limber, son. We ain't out of here, yet"

Chapter 20

Shortly after nightfall, they could see Haskell ahead of them. They rode straight to the boarding house.

"Jeremy, Preacher, where have you been? We've been worried sick." The last was spoken against Jeremy's shoulder, as Elizabeth clung to his neck and showered him with kisses.

"We had a little errand to run, and it took a little while to work it all out," Preacher said. "Mrs. O'Hanlan, would you happen to have enough for the sheriff and his deputy? We've been on the trail all day, and we're a mite hungry!"

"Of course, of course, sit down all of you." Mrs. O'Hanlan bustled around getting more food on the table.

Preacher said, "I just want to thank God for the success of our mission." He bowed his head. "Lord I thank You that You were with us, today. I know You are always with us, but Your hand of protection was very obvious, today. Thank you that no one was hurt, and we were able to do what we went to do. You tell us to pray for our enemies, and I do so, now. Soften their hearts, and give them a desire to know the truth about You. Amen."

"Amen." echoed the men.

"All right, someone please tell me what this is all about," Elizabeth demanded.

"This!" Preacher and Jeremy got up, walked to the door, and brought in the trunk they had left outside on the veranda.

"My trunk," Elizabeth screamed. Then there was a babble as everyone tried to talk at once.

"What? How…?" Elizabeth stammered.

"Jeremy and I thought you should have your trunk and the things in it, so we went to Sheriff Tate for help," explained Preacher. "If it wasn't for him and his deputy, we wouldn't have gotten what we went for. Thomas wasn't going to cooperate until Sheriff Tate convinced him that it was in his best interest."

"Oh, Sheriff, thank you!" Elizabeth exclaimed.

"Shucks, ma'am, we just did what we thought we should do," the sheriff said, obviously embarrassed.

"But wasn't it dangerous? Those people have shown what they really are," observed Mrs. O'Hanlan.

"Well, it was right tense for a few minutes," drawled the sheriff.

"Oh Jeremy, you lovable foolish man! I would rather have you and Preacher safe, than have you risk your lives for this trunk, no matter how dear it is to me. It doesn't even compare to how dear you two are to me," Elizabeth said with tears in her eyes.

"Well, it's done, no one was hurt, and now you can wear your mother's dress for our wedding," Jeremy said. "I can't wait to see you in it."

"Well, you will wait!" said Mrs. O'Hanlan firmly. "Its bad luck for a groom to see his wife's dress before the wedding.

"It's all right, we don't believe in luck. Instead, we believe that God controls everything," Preacher said. "But I agree with Mrs. O'Hanlan, Jeremy. You got to wait until the proper time to see her in that dress."

"Sit down; sit down, while the food is hot. Sheriff, you sit here, deputy here, Jeremy and Preacher, you know your places."

Chapter 21

The trunk had been pried open, there being no key, and Elizabeth and Mrs. O'Hanlan were busily fitting, and tucking and pleating, and whatever else was needed to make the dress just right for the upcoming wedding.

Jeremy and Preacher were busily making their own plans for after the wedding.

"Tell me more about this uncle you have in Ohio and what he wants you to do," Preacher directed.

"Well, Uncle Owen has owned a buggy manufacturing business for years. He custom-makes buggies and harness, and has about 20 employees. He has no son, and has always considered me sort of his substitute son. He has talked in the past, of me taking over his business some day. He has offered to teach me the business by making me his bookkeeper. He says that he would teach me the way he wants it done, not how some Harvard professor thinks it should be done. Once I learn the business well enough, I suppose he will retire from actively operating the business, and I would take over. Elder Thomas always wanted me to introduce him to my uncle, but I never did. Now, I'm glad I didn't."

"Why haven't you started this apprenticeship before? Why were you here with the Brotherhood?" Preacher asked.

"I'm only nineteen. I'll be twenty in March. I heard Elder Thomas speak in Cleveland, and was mesmerized. He said he had God's ear, and spoke for Him. He sounded so believable and rational and I wanted to learn more about the Brotherhood, so I followed him out here. Next thing I knew, I was living in the commune, buying his line. It was only later that I began to question what he was telling the people. It didn't square with what I already knew to be true. Then, when he began to mistreat Elizabeth, I made up my mind. I'm so glad we're both out of there," Jeremy said.

"Why haven't you gone back to Ohio, before now?" Preacher asked.

"I gave Elder Thomas all my money, so I had no way to return. Then, I couldn't leave Elizabeth. We planned to follow the stream that runs through Brotherhood land, to see if we could find a town, and get away that way. But we never had a chance. Elder Thomas kept a close eye on Elizabeth, and I wouldn't leave her."

"Once you're married, what will you do?" Preacher asked.

"I've thought that out," Jeremy replied. We can live here at the boarding house. I will get a job, and save money until we have enough for stagecoach fare. It runs through Cedar City once a week. I'll buy us passage back to Ohio or as close to home as I can get. From there, we'll get home and I'll go see my uncle. I'm sure his offer still holds. Especially, once he meets Elizabeth. He'll love her!"

"Hmm, I'm sure he will," was all Preacher said. "Let's go see if Mrs. O'Hanlan has supper ready."

The next day, Preacher began to make rounds of the town. He could be seen in close, earnest conversation with all the town leaders. Jeremy was too love struck to notice.

Chapter 22

The day of the wedding dawned, snowing hard. No garden wedding this year. Jeremy was nervous at breakfast, and Elizabeth didn't show up at all. The wedding was scheduled for eleven o'clock, so Preacher used the time to go over his charge to the newly-weds, and make sure all was ready.

The parlor had been spit-shined. It was going to be crowded, but Preacher would keep it short, so even those who had to stand wouldn't have to do so for long.

Finally, at half past ten o'clock, guests began to arrive, and Jeremy made his appearance. Where he had found a cut-away coat in this town was more than Preacher could imagine, but there he was, cut-away, cravat and all.

Preacher made his way upstairs, and there was Elizabeth. She was radiant in her mother's dress! She took Preacher's arm. "I'm so happy," she said.

"You're so pretty, I'm not sure I'm going to give you away," Preacher joshed.

"Oh, you say that to all the girls," Elizabeth said, but she was flattered.

"Come on let's show them what they are missing," Preacher grinned.

They descended the stairs, and all eyes were on Elizabeth. Jeremy was pale, but looked proud as a peacock.

Preacher walked Elizabeth up to the front of the room, turned to the guests, and said, "it gives me great pleasure to give Elizabeth Strong to be married this day to Jeremy Maxwell."

The guests all clapped and those who could, sat down.

Preacher passed Elizabeth's hand to Jeremy, and turned to face them. He looked around the room, and noted that everyone had turned out for the great event.

"Before they repeat their vows, I have a few words I want to share as a charge to them. In I Corinthians 13, we're given a description of what real love is, and is not." Here, Preacher read the chapter in its entirety. When he had finished, he said, "That's a tall order, isn't it? True love is not selfish; not proud; not boastful; not arrogant. It never promotes itself at the expense of the other person; in fact, it seeks the good of the other person first. We're told here that it is kind, tolerant, and self-sacrificing, Jeremy, in Ephesians 5:25 men are told to, "love your wife as Christ loves the Church and gave Himself for her." Elizabeth, just before that in that same chapter, verses 22 and 23, Paul says to wives, "Wives submit to your husbands as to the Lord, for the husband is the head of the wife, as Christ is the head of the Church."

"Now if both husband and wife are doing what scripture says they should do, the wife will have no trouble submitting to the husband, since he has her good in mind. The husband won't abuse his headship, since he has the model of Christ's sacrificial love to live up to. I commend you to our Lord's keeping, and wish you the very best in life."

"Now Jeremy, take her by the right hand, and repeat after me."

It was done in minutes, and they were Mr. and Mrs. Jeremy Maxwell.

The guests clapped and cheered, crowding around to offer their congratulations and wish them well. Then Merton Lewis, the merchant, stepped forward.

"Jeremy, Elizabeth, I have been given the pleasant task of presenting a little memento of our esteem." He indicated all the guests with a gesture. "Everyone contributed, and I'm glad to say that we have thirty dollars in gold pieces for you as a gift to help you get started in married life." He handed a small leather bag to Jeremy. "Also, there is a buckboard, harnessed and ready to take you both to Cedar City, after we're done here. Just hand it over to the livery there, and we'll see to getting it back."

"Mr. Lewis, folks, I-I-I don't know what to say. This will get us back to Ohio in fine style, and help us get established there. T-Thank you."

"Glad to do it, son."

"Come on, there's cake and punch," said Mrs. O'Hanlan. "If we get them on their way, they can be in Cedar City yet tonight."

"Preacher, you're behind this, aren't you," said Jeremy, holding up the little bag.

"Well, I had an idea, and talked it over with a few people. They all thought it was a good idea, and acted on it."

"This will let us get back to Ohio, and let me get started learning my uncle's business," Jeremy enthused.

"Oh, it's such an unexpected blessing," Elizabeth chimed in. "You are such a dear man! You have been there for us whenever we've needed you. Jeremy and I have talked it over, and decided to name our first boy after you."

"I'm honored, truly honored," Preacher stammered.

"Well, we can't just call him Preacher, now can we?" Jeremy grinned. "What is your name, anyway?"

Preacher smiled. "Winfield Scott," he said.

"Winfield Scott Maxwell," Elizabeth said. "I like it! Will you come see him sometime?" she asked softly.

"I can't promise but I'll try," said Preacher.

Elizabeth kissed his cheek. "I'll never forget you, you know," she said.

"I know."

They fed each other cake and punch, smearing it all over each other's face, as kids will do.

Then they ran down the steps to the waiting buckboard. The trunk was already tied in the back. Jeremy helped Elizabeth up onto the seat, went around, got into his place and picked up the reins. "Thank you, all." he called. "Goodbye...."

With a rattle of wheels they were off; waving and calling goodbyes.

The townsfolk watched them until they were out of sight then dispersed to their own places.

Chapter 23

"Yep, I've done about all I can do around here, for this time," Preacher said hoisting his bedroll, banjo and possible sack up over Noah's withers. "It's time to be getting on down the trail."

The snow had stopped, and there were about three inches on the ground. It would be cold tonight, and Preacher was glad for the mackinaw he had gotten from Mr. Lewis when he settled up his bill.

"Kids should be in Cedar City, if they didn't have any trouble," observed the sheriff.

"Easily," agreed Preacher.

"You're not going to Cedar City?" the sheriff observed.

"No, I'll cut off about five miles out, and head up over the mountain. There's a logging operation over in West Fork. They need the gospel from what I hear. I'm headin' over that way, at least 'til spring," Preacher said.

"Mind if I ride along a ways?" asked the sheriff.

"No, glad for the company," Preacher responded.

Preacher mounted the old military saddle and pulled the mule around. "Let's go," he said.

As they rode out of town, other eyes watched from some rocks on the ridge. "We ain't done yet, Preacher. Not by a long shot. Some day…" Elder Thomas ground his teeth in frustration.

Of course, Preacher didn't know all this, and if he had, he wouldn't have changed his plans in the least. Elder Thomas and the Brotherhood had been committed to God, and He would take care of it.

The sheriff was pleasant company, and the miles passed quickly. The creak of leather and the sound of hooves on the frozen ground were relaxing. Before Preacher realized it, they were at the cut-off.

"Well, this is where we say goodbye for now," the sheriff said.

"Yes, thanks for the company. By the way, why did you ride out this way with me? Do you have something you need to do before you go back? Can I help you with anything before I go on?" Preacher asked.

"Oh, I just wanted to be sure those skunks didn't see you riding off alone and decide to stink up the air giving you a send-off," the sheriff grinned.

"I thought it might be something like that… thanks," Preacher said.

"When do you expect to be back this way?" the sheriff shifted in his saddle.

"Depends on what I run into, but late spring or early summer, I would think," Preacher responded.

"Good, the people here need you, need to know they can depend on you on a regular basis. I like having you around, too. Who knows, maybe me and Mike will show up at one of your church services. Wouldn't that be a hoot?" the sheriff laughed.

"You know you're always welcome. God doesn't play favorites. He takes us all just like we are. Be glad to see you, anytime." Preacher said earnestly.

"Travel safe," said the sheriff.

"You, too! Best on your retirement," Preacher said.

"Yeah, well I've been thinking that over… What would I do with myself putterin' around in a garden? I'll probably be right here when you come back." Sheriff pulled his horse around and spurred him down the trail before Preacher could respond. He raised his hand in a farewell gesture and disappeared around a bend in the trail.

"Well Noah, just you and me, like always." He turned up the trail toward West Fork

BOOK 2

Chapter 24

The snow got a little deeper, the farther he went. The air was cold, but the sun was bright, so he enjoyed the ride. It was, however slower, so nightfall found him only a little more than about halfway to his destination.

"Looks like another night out under the stars, Noah. Hope it doesn't snow any more," Preacher added.

He found a large boulder off the trail, surrounded by pine trees. *The rock will reflect the heat, and here is plenty of wood for a fire. Don't think I'll find much better.* he mused.

He cut some low-hanging pine boughs and arranged them for his bed. He got his ground cloth, covered the boughs and spread his bedroll on top of it all. He tied Noah in a little opening in the trees, and scraped away the snow so he could get at the few blades of grass available. He took off the saddle, blanket, and hackamore, and hung them in a nearby tree. After wiping Noah down with a bunch of grass, as best he could, he took his possible sack and canteen and set about building a fire.

He knew from experience that the low-hanging dried branches of the pine or fir, makes great tinder, so he gathered as much as he could find. Next he found standing dead wood, broke it off, and since it was dry despite the snow, he soon had a small fire going. He piled the remainder of the wood close to hand, so he could feed the fire all through the night, as he wished.

Reaching into his possible sack, he pulled out a piece of jerky, took a drink from his canteen, and bit off a piece of the jerky. Not the first night he had gone without a hot meal, so he was content. The fire was warming the rock, which was reflecting the heat onto his back; *not bad, not bad at all!* His eyes grew heavy.

Suddenly there was a sound. Something alien to the sounds of the forest he was accustomed to. "Hello, out there. Come on in, you're welcome," he called.

No answer, no further sound, nothing. He got up and went out to check on Noah. If it was a predator of some kind, he had no way to defend himself.

Noah was standing, ears forward, looking into the forest. He had heard it, too. Preacher patted him and spoke low into his ear. Noah's head dropped, and he began to nibble at the sparse grass again. Whatever it was, it was gone now.

"Lord," Preacher prayed, "I don't know what or who is out here with us, but You do. Neither do I know their intentions, but my trust is in You. I would pray for safety, but Your will is what I really want. If there is something You are trying to show me, make it plain. Amen."

Preacher stayed with Noah for half an hour or more. Nothing else disturbed the calm. Noah continued to peacefully nibble the grass. Finally, Preacher went back to his bed, but he didn't sleep soundly. Every few minutes, he would awaken, listen for a while, perhaps stoke the fire, and then doze off again. About midnight, he went back to check on Noah.

Still the same, Noah didn't give any sign that there was anything or anyone in the area. Preacher finally went back to his bedroll.

At morning's first light, Preacher was up. He got out some biscuits Mrs. O'Hanlan had insisted on him taking. Munching on them, and taking a drink from his canteen, he began to break camp. He rolled up his bedroll and the ground cloth. He made sure the camp fire was dead out, covering it with dirt and snow. Then he went back to where Noah was tied. There he was, still giving no sign that anything was around. Preacher saddled him, and put on the hackamore. He slung his bedroll, possible sack, canteen, and banjo over Noah's withers and mounted the saddle. He pulled Noah's head around and nudged him into movement, forgetting all about last night and whatever it was that went bump in the night.

He headed toward the trail, and hitting it, turned to continue to West Fork. He froze, an involuntary chill running down his back. There crossing the trail were boot tracks!

It hadn't been his imagination, and it hadn't been an animal on the prowl. Why hadn't whoever it was, come into his camp at his greeting, shared his fire, and swapped a few stories? Obviously, the nocturnal visitor had not wanted to be seen, so at Preacher's hail, he had hot-footed it out of the area. Not a real good sign... "Lord, I know You always protect me, but this time, thank You for your special hand on Noah and me."

Preacher nudged Noah in the flanks, and moved on up the trail.

Late that afternoon, Preacher saw the pall of smoke from the drying kilns over the valley, and knew that he was coming into West Fork.

Chapter 25

West Fork was even less impressive than Haskell, although it was bigger. Here, there were few permanent buildings, with most dwellings being tents. Oh, there were a few buildings; the general store; the school house; the livery; the sheriff's office and jail; the sawmill office; the train depot. Otherwise, it was a town of tents. Even the mandatory saloon was a large open tent with tables and chairs set out under a canvas tarp.

The main street was all but impassible. Horses hooves, wagon wheels, and logs being skidded to the sawmill, combined with the snow and wet, had churned the street into a bog that pedestrian traffic could not even attempt to cross from one side of the street to the other, except at one place where sawed planks had been lain across the mud to form a slippery precarious bridge, of sorts.

People, wagons, and horse teams were everywhere. It was indeed bustling, Preacher noted. He sat on a knoll just outside of town, overlooking the activity and wondering if he was up to the task the Lord had called him to. It was a daunting sight.

"Lord, this looks impossible to me. I'm not at all sure I can get Noah down Main Street, and look at all these people. It looks like an ant pile. I don't know if there is a boarding house, I don't see one, and yet. Lord, You're the God of the impossible. Your strength is made perfect in my weakness, and even though I don't feel adequate, You are, so You take over. These people need Your Word. May I be faithful. Amen."

Preacher rode down off the knoll, into town. *Best place to start is at the sheriff's office,* he thought to himself.

Riding around the back of the "buildings" facing Main Street, he soon found the sheriff's office and jail. Hitching Noah, he went around to the front door and entered the office.

The sheriff looked up from a stack of wanted posters he was reading through. "Now, what can I do for you?" he queried.

"My name's Winfield Scott. I'm a circuit riding preacher, come to establish a work here," Preacher said.

"A preacher?" the sheriff cried. "A preacher?"

"I just stopped by to get the lay of the land from you. Since you're the sheriff…"

"A preacher? You've got to be kidding, right? What's the punch line?"

"No punch line, Sheriff. I thought that since you were sheriff and all, you would know where the boarding house is, who I need to see about setting up and holding Sunday services, and who the important people are in town, so I can talk to them and try to get their support for what I'm going to be doing," Preacher explained.

"A preacher! Who'd have thought? Don't you know what kind of town this is?" the sheriff asked.

"Well, no I don't know much about it except that it's a lumber town."

"A lumber town, do you know what that means?" the sheriff asked more calmly.

"Lumberjacks cut down trees, which are brought to the sawmill by some means, cut up into lumber, dried in a kiln, and shipped out by train to customers," Preacher said seriously.

"It's a toss up as to which is tougher, a gold strike town or a lumbering town," the sheriff said wearily. "I have four deputies. We have all we can handle to break up the fights, and keep some semblance of peace here. I'm afraid you've come to the wrong place. There are far greener pastures elsewhere, parson. I wish it were different, but that's the truth," the sheriff sagged back into his chair.

"What you've told me is exactly the reason the Lord sent me here," Preacher exclaimed. "These people need Jesus in order for real change to take place."

"You mean you want to stay?" The sheriff couldn't believe what he was hearing.

"Well, yes. That's why I came," Preacher responded.

"You're crazy!" the sheriff exploded.

"Maybe, but my God isn't, and He sent me over here. So, any help you can give me to get started, would be greatly appreciated by me, and may have an impact on the problem you have as well," Preacher said earnestly.

"Well, it's your funeral... so to speak," the sheriff was embarrassed. "You'd better go see Hiz'onor the Mayor... that is, if he's sober. This time of day, it's a toss up He has so many problems with no solutions, that usually by this time of day, he's out of it, or at least well on his way. Name's Ray Black, you'll find him in the last tent on this side of Main Street. Have you seen it? That's one of his insolvable problems. With the first snow, Main Street became Main Pig Sty, and has only gotten worse."

Preacher nodded.

"There's no boarding house. The one that was here got turned into the general store, after the last lumberjacks tore it up during one of their fights. Owner said, 'No more', and closed 'er up. Ask the mayor, there's an extra room in back of the school house. Maybe he'll let you stay there, since we don't have no school master. Hey… that's a good idea. Maybe you could be the school master and solve one of his biggest headaches for him."

"I'm no school teacher," Preacher said, shaking his head.

"Well, as a parson, you can read, write, and cipher, can't you?"

"Yes, but…"

"No buts! The mayor has a real big problem on his hands with the school kids. You solve that one for him, and you could own this town," the sheriff stated positively. "Well, you do what you want to do. You asked me for my help, and I'm telling you that you're gonna have a rough go of it pushing religion around here."

"Not religion, Jesus is…"

"I don't care how you slice it, it's gonna be a hard sell," said the sheriff. "Take it from me."

"I'll keep it in mind. You think the mayor is there, now." Preacher asked?

"Sure, he's there. He stays there. He just does his mayor business there, whenever it's needed," the sheriff stated positively.

"All right, guess I'd just as well go see him now, and see if I can camp somewhere." Preacher got to his feet.

"All right, but take it from me, you're missing a bet if you don't talk to him about that school master job. Come back and see me. I brew a mean pot of coffee, and you're interestin' to talk to." The sheriff turned back to his posters.

Preacher walked out and was almost run over by a nice looking lady in rancher garb who was half running and out of breath. "Sheriff, they're at it…" Preacher excused himself and continued on out to Noah.

Busy man, he thought.

Preacher mounted Noah and rode on down the line of tents and buildings, until he got to the last tent in town. There being no hitching post, he ground-hitched Noah and went around to the tent flap. *Noah's been ground-hitched many times, he won't wander off.* Preacher thought. "Anyone here?" he called.

"Who wants to know?" called a slurred voice.

"I'm Winfield Scott, circuit riding preacher of the Gospel of Our Lord Jesus Christ. I would like to talk to you, please," said Preacher.

"Well, come on in."

Preacher entered the tent. The mayor was sitting behind a small desk, his feet on a box, and a glass in his hand. "It's that time in the afternoon, when I usually knock off, kick back and relax," Ray Black explained. "I don't usually get official visitors this late in the day. Drink?"

"No, no thanks. I don't drink," Preacher said.

"Oh? Uh, of course." The mayor set his drink on the box and got up, extending his hand. "Ray Black. I'm mayor around here."

"Yes, I talked to the sheriff and he told me where to find you. I just got into town, and would like to establish Sunday services for the residents around here, as well as to help with any spiritual needs they might have. I will need use of a place large enough to accommodate however many might attend the services," explained Preacher.

"Well now, that's fine, mighty fine. I know this town could do with a little religious influence. It's a little rough around the edges, so to speak. I know the town leaders are all for bringing a little more culture and refinement to the town. It would be a good start to have a little religion," the mayor was hedging, and Preacher let him wind down.

"I'm not talking about religion, Mr. Mayor. I'm talking about the life-changing Gospel message of salvation and redemption. I'm talking about God reaching down into this community and changing lost men and women," said Preacher.

"Uh, yes, of course. I understand. But we have several problems we'll have to work out." The mayor was starting to squirm.

"What might those problems be, sir? I'll be happy to begin working on them right away," Preacher said.

"Well," the mayor said, "to begin with, there is no place to accommodate your, uh parishioners."

"In the past, where there has been no church building, I have worked out a deal with the local saloon to use their facilities on Sunday morning. Since they can't legally sell alcoholic beverages from Saturday midnight, until Sunday at sundown, they have been happy to let me use their halls. I can go talk with them about the possibility. Who do I need to contact?" Preacher kept the pressure on.

"Well, Tom Grady owns the saloon, but it is only a tent, and the tables are outside under a canvas. I'm afraid it is not suitable for your purposes," the mayor smiled.

"I saw it on my way into town. I think we can work out something that will do just fine." Preacher sat down on a nail keg that served as a chair.

"Well, if you think so…"

"What other problem do you see?" Preacher asked.

"Uh, well, uh, uh…" Between the effects of the whisky, and being put on the spot, Hiz'onor was having a hard time with these negotiations. "Some people may be offended, and this is a rough town. I don't want to see you get hurt."

"Offended at what?" Preacher asked. "I don't intend to collar anyone, or force people to come to services."

"Well, there are some rough lumberjacks in this town…" the mayor said lamely.

"Of more immediate concern, is the fact that I have been told there is no boarding house here in town. Is there a place I can camp, or some other arrangement I can make?" Preacher asked.

The mayor brightened up. "Of course, there is no place for you to stay. Say that's too bad, because I think the town could really use your services."

"I'm used to staying outside," Preacher said, "but there is a problem of cleaning up, with no water."

"Yes, there is that," said the mayor.

"The sheriff mentioned a room in back of the school house. He said that since you have no school master, it was empty, and to ask you about the possibility of renting it from the town," Preacher said hopefully.

It was as if the whisky fumes all fled the mayor's head, and his eyes took on a shrewd look.

Chapter 26

"Say, that's right," he exclaimed. "Maybe we could help each other. You could be the answer to a real big problem that I haven't been able to solve."

Preacher's heart lurched. He knew what was coming. "I don't know anything about fixing your Main Street problem," he said desperately.

"Oh, not that," said the mayor, "but another problem I have could be solved. You see, we have a school house here in town. We have had three school masters, one woman, and two men. None has stayed for a complete school year. The woman came closest. You see, the children are… I'm afraid… rather unruly, and have run all of them off before the year was out. We had an agreement with a Mr. Harvey Banks. He showed up in late August to prepare for the school year. He stayed exactly one week, until the next train came in, and walked out! He didn't even try; he just heard the stories and walked out. The children haven't had school all term, because we haven't been able to find another school master."

"I'm sorry, Mr. Mayor. I can't help you. I'm not a school teacher," said Preacher.

"You can however, read?"

"Yes."

"Write?"

"Yes."

"Do sums?"

"Yes…but I'm not a teacher."

"No buts. Our first teachers in this country were clergymen who saw a need to educate the people. You will do splendidly. There is a box of McGuffy readers, slates and chalk, all left by our Mr. Banks. The town will pay you the same wages as a top lumberjack, ten dollars a month, and you can stay in the school house. It has a stove and a pump for water. You can even use it for your Sunday church services." The mayor was warming to his topic now.

"Thank you, but I can't," Preacher said.

"Why not? Aha, I see you drive a hard bargain. All right, I admit we're in a hard way. We'll double the money, and put in some pots and pans, dishes and tableware, so you will be comfortable."

"That's not it," said Preacher. "I've never taught school. I don't know the first thing about it."

"So what? You're better than what we have now. Just teach the little b… uh dears to read, write, and cipher numbers," the mayor argued. Then he played his hole card. "Besides, you want to minister here, don't you? This is the only way you can stay here and do that."

"Ouch!" Preacher was had, and he knew it. It wasn't a bad arrangement. He could do his ministry and have support while doing it. But they had run off three other school masters, so it wasn't going to be a Sunday afternoon walk by the lake. Preacher tried one more time. "Look, Mr. Mayor suppose I try it on an interim basis, until you can get a genuine school master. You keep looking for one, and I'll stay on until he or she gets here, or until the end of the school year, whichever comes first."

"Agreed!" said the mayor, and grinned. "Here is the key to the school house. I'll send some men over tomorrow, to furnish it so you will be comfortable. And just to show you that I am a good sort, we'll pay you for the entire month, even though it is almost half gone. Come by tomorrow, and I'll pay you the first month's wages. Oh, we'll start classes on the fifteenth." He held out his hand. Preacher shook it.

"Lord, what have you gotten me into, this time? I wanted to minister here, but it looks like all I'll be doing is babysitting." Then like a thunderbolt, it hit him. "I have a captive congregation. What an opportunity! Just figure out how to minister to them. Thank you, Lord. What a fool I am. This was Your plan all along!" Then his prayer changed. "Lord help me know how to effectively minister to these young lives You are entrusting to me."

Preacher walked outside, and climbed aboard Noah, in a daze of thinking about how to approach this new challenge he had just accepted. He headed toward the whitewashed school house on the knoll in the distance.

As he opened the door of the school house, the mice scattered. *Gonna have to move them out,* he thought. Light filtered through the shuttered windows, so he could see, although poorly.

Just inside the door was a small coat room, where the children could leave their coats, lunches and anything else they brought for the day. Beyond that was a larger room full of benches. A pot-bellied stove in the back, next to the coat room, served to heat the room. *Plenty of wood-chopping to serve as disciplinary chores,* Preacher thought. On the front wall was a slate board. Surprisingly, it was fairly smooth.

Just to the left of the slate, as he faced it, was a door. Preacher opened the door, and found himself in the head master's quarters. *Not much, but it will do*, Preacher thought. It contained a well-used cot and a small cupboard. To the right, was another door leading to what appeared to be a small kitchen area. It contained another cupboard, a basin, a hand pump, which needed priming before it would pump water, a small cook stove for heat as well as cooking he knew, a table with one broken leg, and two chairs. *In case I have company*, he thought. A plank floor throughout was a luxury he didn't think he would have, but a welcome one.

He opened the kitchen cupboard, and found a kerosene lamp with some oil it, so he lit the lamp and the room took on a rosy glow. *Looks better in this light*, he mused.

He went back outside to take care of Noah, and bring in his meager possessions. A lean- to on the back of the building was evidently used for wood. It was empty now, so Preacher tied Noah under the slanting roof, unsaddled him, took off the hackamore, and gathered some of the grass growing along the building for him. "I'll take better care of you, tomorrow, old fella," Preacher promised. "This will have to do for tonight."

He carried his bedroll, ground cloth, possible sack, banjo, and canteen into the school house and back to his room. He spread the ground cloth on top of the straw ticking on the cot, and spread his bedroll on top of the ground cloth. He propped his banjo in the corner of the room, then got into his possible sack and pulled out a piece of jerky and sat down on the cot. Chewing methodically, and drinking from his canteen, Preacher began to consider the situation he found himself in.

"Lord, You know that these youngsters are liable to eat me alive. They've done it to three other school masters, and they were experienced teachers. They're probably already planning how to get rid of me. You brought me to this place to represent You, and spread Your Gospel. It appears that the only way I'm going to be able to do that, is to deal with teaching these children. I need Your wisdom and guidance pretty bad. Not only do I want to teach them their ABCs, but I want to impact them for You. Please show me what to do. Amen."

He pulled off his boots, shirt and pants, lay back on the cot, and pulled his bedroll over him. In moments he was asleep.

Chapter 27

Next morning at daylight, he was awakened by Noah sounding off for his breakfast. "All right, old fella. I told you I would take care of you today, and I will." He shrugged into his shirt, pulled on his pants, and knocked out his boots from habit before putting them on.

"Come on," he went outside and sure enough, Noah had made short work of the grass he had gathered the night before. Preacher saddled him, and put on the hackamore, then taking the reins he led Noah toward the main street, looking for a way across, since the livery was on the other side, of course. He ended up leading the mule all the way to the edge of town where he could gingerly pick his way across to the other side, then back uptown to the livery stable. The stable man took Noah back to a stall, talking to him all the way. "Yeah, we'll get along," he said when he came back. "You're the new school master, eh," he observed.

"Word sure gets around fast," said Preacher wryly.

"Yep, nothing much gets by around here," the stable man observed. "My name's Ed." He stuck out his hand, and Preacher shook it.

"Well, with no boarding house around here, where can a man get some breakfast?" Preacher asked.

"Sadie'll fix you right up," said Ed. "You just need to get back across the street, and… see that big canvas top with the tables and benches underneath?" He pointed several tents down on the other side of the street. "That's it. Best place in town… mainly 'cause it's the only place in town." He guffawed at his own humor.

"Thanks, Ed. Guess I'll go give it a try." Preacher moved off before Ed could launch another of his knee-slappers. He walked down what would have been the sidewalk or boardwalk, if there had been a sidewalk or boardwalk. With it being early morning, and the ground still somewhat frozen, when he came to the poor excuse for a pedestrian crossing, he decided to chance it. He stepped gingerly out onto the planks, and moved quickly to the other side. *I wouldn't chance it later in the day*, he thought.

He walked on down to the tent Ed had pointed out as Sadie's café, diner, or whatever she called it The place was pretty full. "Just find an empty spot at a table, and I'll be right with you, hon" sang out a woman who would outweigh Noah by a good bit.

Preacher nodded and moved to an empty chair he spotted in the corner. As he sank into the chair, the woman breezed up. "Ham and eggs, and all the biscuits, gravy and coffee you want. Two bits."

Preacher raised his eyebrows, and the woman caught the gesture. "When you're the only show in town, you do your own thing. Tell you what, you being the new school master and all, I'll cut you a special deal. Fifteen cents, and if you come regular like, it'll always be half price for you."

"Deal!" Preacher said, not at all liking the idea of having to cook his own meals. "Let me ask you something. Does everyone already know about me being the new school master?"

"Why, sure. We all knew last night after you accepted the mayor's offer," she smiled. "Welcome to West Fork," she said sweetly.

"All right, can I substitute for the ham? I'm not particularly fond of ham. Sausage would suit me better," Preacher inquired.

"Not here honey, we cook one thing. If you want it, you get it, if you don't, you pass. Tonight will be smoked sausage, grits, greens, apple pie and coffee. What's your pleasure?"

"I'll have the breakfast, and I'll see you, tonight," Preacher stated positively.

"Thought you might," she observed. "Not much for cookin', are you?"

Preacher just grinned, "Caught again!"

After breakfast, Preacher walked back down to the mayors, office. "Ya in, Your Honor?" Preacher called out.

"I'm always in, come on in," the mayor responded. "Guess you had your breakfast, how was it?"

"Do you all know when I use the privy, too?" Preacher frowned. "I feel sort of like an ant under a glass."

"Well, it'll die down in a few days. Right now, you're a novelty, an answer to our prayers... so to speak," the mayor said hastily. "Here!" He tossed a small leather pouch to Preacher. I told you I would have your first month's pay ready for you. There it is. I was going to give it to you as a twenty dollar gold piece, but I thought the other townspeople might have trouble changing it whenever you buy something. So I broke it down. The largest is a five dollar gold piece. Hope it's all right."

"Just fine, Mayor, just fine," Preacher smiled.

"I'm sending some men out to fill your wood box, bring some pots, pans, and dishes, making sure you're all settled in."

"Mighty fine of you, Mayor. Could I make one request?" Preacher asked.

"Sure, what is it?" asked the Mayor.

"Lights. When the weather is good, we will have the shutters open and light is no problem. There is a kerosene lamp for my use back in my room, but when the weather is bad, and the shutters must be closed, the children need to be able to see what they are doing."

"Of course,." the mayor responded. "We had lamps in the school room, before. But the children broke most of them so we took what were left out. I'll have the men bring lamps back out to the school room, and install them for you."

"Then I think we're all set. I found the readers. Mice have chewed a couple of them, but they're usable…"

"Of course, I forgot the cat," the mayor interrupted. We always had a cat out there. I know where there is a new litter of kittens. I'll get a cat out there, this week. You won't have to worry about feeding it. It'll stay fat on the mice it catches."

"How many students should I expect?" Preacher asked.

"Last year, there were thirteen. If they all come back, I would expect you will have thirteen again. You're not superstitious, are you?" the mayor chuckled.

"No, I'm not superstitious. God controls everything, so superstition and chance have no place in the life of a Christian."

"Yes, of course you're right." The mayor shuffled some paper on his desk.

"About Sunday services in the school house, could I start this Sunday?" Preacher asked

"I don't see why not. Don't be discouraged though, if you don't get many people."

"I won't. That's God's part; I just have to be ready to do my part. See you in the service, Mayor?" Preacher asked.

"What? Ahh, well, we'll see." The mayor was having all he could do to keep from passing out at the thought.

Preacher bid him good day, and took his leave. He decided to see what the general store had to offer, so he turned in that direction. Entering, he saw a sign proudly advertising "Mercantile" and was struck by the feeling of permanence of a building, contrasted to the tent which served as the mayor's office. This was a place of business, and felt like it.

Harvey and Ida Burke were the proprietors of the business. They were both present and ready to help him when he entered. "Hello, Mr. School Master, welcome to our General Store. What can we do for you?"

"Well, I'm just out looking the town over to get an idea of what is here, and I thought I'd drop in and get acquainted with you folks. I do have need for some poster board and paint, however," Preacher said.

"I don't have much call for those kinds of things, but what I do have is right over here." said Harvey.

Preacher selected a piece of poster board, and a quill pen and India ink instead of paint. "If I letter a poster for Sunday services, will you let me display it in your window where people can see it?" Preacher asked.

"Of course, be happy to do so," said Harvey. "But I thought you were a school teacher. Are you a preacher, too?"

"I'm a preacher first and school teacher second," responded Preacher. "I'll have this back to you this afternoon."

He bid the Burkes goodbye and headed for the school house. For the next half hour, he lettered his poster.

Sunday Service

10:00 AM All Welcome

School House

It took longer for the India ink to dry where it would not smudge, than to letter the poster. About one o'clock the mayor's men showed up with all that the mayor had promised, except a cat. "He's taking care of that, himself," they said.

After they were finished, Preacher took the poster back to the Mercantile. "We'll hang it right on the door, so that anyone who comes in will be sure to see it," Ida directed.

On Sunday, Preacher was ready and waiting outside the door of the school house. Ten o'clock came and went with no one showing up. He tried to say, "Well, I guess that's the way You want it, Lord," but his heart wasn't in it. He was down, and with the first day of school coming on Monday, he had to admit that he wasn't sure he was ready.

Chapter 28

A t eight forty-five on Monday morning, Preacher was waiting in front of the school house door. As the students arrived, he greeted each one. Sure enough, when they were all in place, there were thirteen students.

"Eddie Carver was going to come, but his dad needs him at the ranch," he was told.

"Boys and girls, young ladies and gentlemen, my name is Winfield Scott. You can call me Mr. Scott or Teacher whichever you prefer. I came across the mountain from Haskell to be your school master the rest of this year. I know that half of the school year is already gone. We will pick up as though it was back in September, and we'll do as much as we can in the time we have left in this school year."

"There is a wide range in your ages, and some of you have had more schooling than others, so I will try to tailor your school work to your age and experience. Some of the work will be, of necessity, repetition and boring to some of you. I will try to keep that to a minimum. You, in the back there, Tommy, isn't it? You appear to be the oldest in class. How old are you Tommy?"

"Fifteen, teacher," came the response.

"And you twins, how old are you?" Preacher asked.

"Seven, Mr. Scott."

"How many of you live in town?" Preacher looked around the room as most of the hands went up.

"And who comes farthest to school?"

All hands pointed to a ten year old boy. "How far do you come, son?" Preacher asked.

"Seven miles, sir. I ride my pony, Peachy."

"That's a great name. Why do you call her Peachy?" Preacher asked.

"'Cause she's a peach," the boy grinned. "She'll do anything I ask her to do

"And what's your name?" Preacher asked.

"Pete, sir… Pete Tanner."

"All right Pete, thank you." Preacher looked around the room. "Do you see?" he asked. "We're all different, with different backgrounds, different feelings, and different ideas. I'm different from each of you, just as you are different from me. But we're all here because we have a job to do. My job is to teach you what you need to know to get along in this world as an adult. Your job is to learn as much as you possibly can, so when you see a notice posted, for example, you will be able to know what it says, or when you buy something, you will know if you got the correct change back."

"I pledge to teach you the best I possibly can, but I need your help. I've heard the stories about how you have run off the other school masters you have had."

There was a general stir. Students looked at each other and shuffled around. *What is coming next?* they wondered.

"You have quite a reputation, and qualified teachers have refused to deal with it, so they just won't come here. That's why school is just now starting for the year."

"It wouldn't start at all, if we had our way," called Tommy. Laughter broke out, and a few, "yeah, yeahs" reached Preacher's ears.

He ignored them and continued. "This school room is a community, just as the town is a community of people who have come together for a common purpose. Our purpose is learning, their purpose is to harvest the timber in this area and cut and ship the lumber from it. Whatever the community's purpose is, it can only be achieved as its members agree to operate by rules set up to make everything run smoothly. A town or territory calls these rules laws. I have spent the last three days thinking and praying about what rules to set up for our community. I'm sure your other school masters have had their ideas, and set up their own set of rules."

"Yeah, and some of them were pretty stupid, if you ask me," said a boy over by the stove, sarcastically.

Preacher continued, "As I thought about this, I realized that being new in town, and to this school, I am handicapped by not knowing what happens day to day. So my rules may be wrong or inadequate to meet the needs of this school room. Therefore, I've decided to take a different approach. You all are going to make the rules, and you will run the school."

"What?" The children couldn't believe what they had heard! They came halfway out of their seats in disbelief.

"That's right," Preacher said. "I will write the rules on the slate, as you create them. When we are done, I'll make a poster of all the rules, and post it to remind us all what they are."

There was silence as the children looked at each other in confusion. They shuffled and gave each other blank looks. This was not the way other school masters had operated. They had made the rules, and the children had done whatever it took to get around, break, and generally destroy those rules.

"Come on," Preacher invited, "who'll be first? We'll discuss each rule, and if everyone agrees that it is a good rule, I'll write it on the slate."

More coughing, shuffling, and general stir.

"This is our lesson for today. We have all day to do it, and no one may go out to recess or go home until we get it done," Preacher insisted.

Finally, one of the twins spoke up from the front row. "Teacher, whenever us little kids go out to recess, the bigger boys come and push us out of the swings and take them away from us. That's not right. We should make a rule about that."

"Fine," said Preacher. "What do the rest of you think about that?"

"Well, there are only four swings, and they want to hog them." This comment led to a lively discussion which resulted in the first rule. "No bullying."

Preacher wrote it on the blackboard, No bullying. "That's a good start. Let's take a short recess and think about other good rules. We'll continue this when we come back in fifteen minutes."

There was an animated buzz as the children got up and headed for the door. Preacher bowed his head and prayed, "Thank you Lord, for the idea. It seems to be working. I think they're all involved and excited about the exercise. Help them to all buy into the idea, and abide by the rules, so we can have a good school term. Amen."

When Preacher stuck his head out the door and called, "recess is over." they all came trouping back into the school room, rosy cheeked from the cold air, and eyes sparkling with excitement.

Rules came faster, now. "No cheating, no lying, no fighting, no stealing." One of the older girls said, "I think we should have a rule that we have to wipe our feet when we come in from outside. Look at the mess we've made on the floor."

Preacher intervened. "Remember," he said, "we have to live day to day with the rules we make. So we should have a few important rules, not a bunch of rules that become more of a nuisance than a help."

When they finally ran down, Preacher had a list of eight rules on the blackboard. They were: No bullying; Respect others and their opinions; Help each other; No cheating; No lying; No fighting; No swearing; No stealing.

"You've made some good rules, they're important, and you've all agreed on them, but we're not done, yet. Rules have to have consequences. They are no good unless something happens when you break them. In town, if you break a law, the sheriff puts you in jail, or the judge makes you pay a fine. We have to decide what happens if someone breaks these rules" Preacher explained.

More shuffling and blank looks. No one wanted to commit… to be the one who dropped the hammer.

Finally Tommy said, "These are all serious rules, and they should have serious penalties. If someone bullies a smaller person, they should have to apologize to that person, and chop a box of firewood for the teacher."

"More than one," came a voice. "Yeah, for a week," said another.

"Do you all agree?" asked Preacher.

"Yeah, yeah that's good," they all agreed.

"And if you don't show respect or listen to another person, you should have to find out why he or she thinks what they do, and make a report to teacher explaining their viewpoint."

Oh, that's good, Preacher thought.

"If you won't help someone who needs help, you should have to help teacher an hour each day after class, for a week."

"If you are caught fighting, you should have to be tied together with whoever you're fighting, and be with them all day that way."

"If you swear, you should get your mouth washed out with lye soap."

"No, that's what my mom does and it doesn't work."

And so it went

"If you cheat, you should get a black mark for the day, and have to bring your mom or dad in to talk to Mr. Scott."

Finally, they were down to the last two; no lying and no stealing.

"Those are the most serious of our rules." said Tommy. "I think breaking those deserves black max." There was a sharp intake of breath from most of the children.

"Black max?" Preacher queried, "I don't understand what you're talking about."

"Black max!" insisted Tommy. "Right there over the blackboard."

Preacher turned again to the blackboard, and noted again the six foot, blacksnake whip that hung coiled over the blackboard. It was a deadly, evil-looking thing that Preacher had wondered about when he first saw it.

"Well, now I'm not sure that would be appropriate..."

A babble of voices rose, interrupting what he was going to say. Everyone was trying to talk at once!

"Wait, wait, one at a time," Preacher called.

"Mr. Leopold used to threaten to use that on us, when he was here," an older girl said.

"Those rules are the most important. A severe penalty will insure that no one will break them," another boy said.

"I'm scared of it," said another.

"Well, I'm not in favor of whipping or threatening students with it," said Preacher. "I was going to take that thing out of here, but I just forgot and haven't done it, yet."

"Well," Tommy said, "the sight of it hanging there should give us all a reminder of what happens to liars and thieves."

"Yeah, leave it up there," they all urged.

"All right, you win," Preacher said, "But we need to state specifically what the penalty will be for breaking each of these rules."

"If you're caught lying, three stripes on the bare back with Black Max."

"Stealing is the lowest thing you can do. If you are caught stealing, it should be ten stripes on the bare back with Black Max."

Preacher shook his head. "I'm not in favor of this, but I said you are in charge of the school. Is this what you want?"

"Yeah, yeah, this is good. This will help us have a great school year. No one will try to break *these* rules!"

"All right," Preacher said, "good job! School is dismissed."

They stood up as one and headed for the door, laughing and talking gaily.

Preacher got out his poster board, and began lettering.

Chapter 29

Next day, the snow storm hit. Snow was blowing horizontally across the landscape, into massive snow drifts. The old schoolhouse shook as the wind hit it. The snow drifted against the east side of the building, getting deeper and deeper until there was just a little light seeping in around the shutters. And cold! The pot bellied stove barely kept up with it.

In spite of the conditions, the students showed up for school; all but ten-year-old Pete Tanner. A seven mile ride in this weather was more than anyone should tackle, and Preacher supposed that he had stayed home because of it.

Preacher broke out the readers and began having the children read aloud, so he could assess their reading skills. The girls read pretty well, with one girl reading as well as he himself did. The boys were a mixed bag. One of the younger boys read pretty well, but several of the older boys struggled mightily.

Mid morning found Preacher feeling that he had a good handle on the reading skills of his students, and he had the children pass in the readers. The back row of children turned on their benches, peering at the door. Then Preacher heard it. What he had thought to be the wind was a voice calling for help. He shrugged into his mackinaw and opened the door. There was Pete Tanner! He had come to school after all, but he had paid a severe price for his dedication. He was almost frozen on the back of Peachy. He couldn't even speak coherently. Preacher stuck his head back inside the school house calling, "Tommy, get your coat on and come help me." Then he went back to Pete's side and began trying to break loose the ice that had formed all down Pete's right side.

Between Preacher and Tommy, they got Pete inside the school house and put him as close to the stove as they dared. Preacher thought that if he had frostbite, the heat wouldn't be good for him, but they needed to get him warmed up. School lessons were forgotten as the children tried to do what they could to help. Water pooled around Pete as the ice melted from his clothes.

"Why did you do it, Pete? Why did you come to school in this storm? It's a wonder you're alive. Only God preserved you." Preacher shook his head in wonder.

"I wanted to see how our rules were working out," Pete croaked. He managed a wry smile, "besides a little snow doesn't stop the Tanners."

"Well, there are our rules, lettered on poster board and tacked on the wall next to the slateboard. How do they look?" Preacher asked.

"Great! Would someone please take care of Peachy for me? She's the one that got me here. She's the best pony ever," Pete said earnestly, his eyes filling.

"I'll do it," Tommy said, and got up to do it.

Pete was now starting to relax a little, as the heat was working its wonders. Preacher examined his hands and cheeks for signs of white spots indicating frostbite, but found none.

"You sit there and dry out a little bit,." he directed Pete. "The rest of you, we're going to have a spell down. Number off by twos, starting with you, Mary."

"One, two, one, two..."

"All right, ones on this side of the room, twos on that side. I'll give you each a word to spell. If you get it right, you remain standing, if you miss it, you sit down. All right Mary, your first word is..."

"Wait! What team am I on? I'm a good speller, and since I'm here, I want to play, too!" Pete was all belligerent, his chin jutting out, and his face red.

"All right, Pete," Preacher soothed, "I thought you'd just want to sit and rest a while. If you want to join in, you are welcome. You would be a one, so join those students."

Preacher made a mental note, *hot temper, so watch him.*

The spell down went until lunch time, with one of the older girls being the last one standing. Lydia blushed and was obviously pleased to have won the contest.

"All right, it's time for lunch. You'll have to stay in here today, I'm afraid," Preacher said. "We'll start class again promptly at one-fifteen." There was a general stir as the children rose to go to the coatroom to retrieve their lunches.

Preacher noted that eleven-year-old Johnny Jamison didn't move with the rest of the students. In spite of not being the youngest boy in class, he was noticeably the smallest boy. That combined with the way he dressed, separated him from the other students, and he didn't seem to have any friends. The students were friendly to him, and didn't shun him, but neither did they go out of their way to befriend him.

He always wore overalls and a suit coat that was too large for him. It appeared to be a man's suit coat that had been cut down for him to wear, and none too well at that. It was held together with a large safety pin in front, and Johnny never took it off.

Preacher saw him looking around uncertainly, and knew what he had to do.

"Johnny, would you please come up here? I need your help," Preacher called out.

Johnny came up to the front of the room. "What do you want?" he asked.

"Sadie sent up my lunch, but I don't know what she was thinking. She sent this huge sandwich, a bowl of soup, an apple, and this big piece of cake. If I eat all of this, I'll fight sleep all afternoon. I noticed that you had finished your lunch already, and thought that maybe you would help me out with some of this. If I just throw it out, and she gets wind of it, she may not like it, and I don't want to make the cook mad!" Preacher stole a look at Johnnie. He was looking longingly at the food.

"Sure, I mean… I guess so. If you're sure you don't want it." Johnnie couldn't keep his eyes off the lunch.

"Let me cut the sandwich in half and I'll give you half of the soup. You can have the apple and half of the cake. If you can eat half, it will sure help me out," Preacher said as he began cutting the sandwich in half.

"I think I can do that," Johnnie said grinning.

Preacher divided the soup and the cake. "Here, you can sit at the side of my desk, if you want to. I sure appreciate you doing this for me."

"It's all right, I got room," Johnnie said around a bite of sandwich.

Note: *Watch this situation. It may not be the only time he needs help*, Preacher thought..

After the food was gone, Johnnie wandered off to find something to do until class resumed. Some of the students were playing a game Preacher had never seen. Others were sitting in a circle talking together animatedly. Johnnie joined the circle, and Preacher soon forgot about him, and began to plan for ciphering, which was the next subject to tackle. He began to write sample problems on the slate.

Precisely at one-fifteen, Preacher called the students back to class. They came willingly enough, even though they had not been able to get outside to work off some energy.

"All right, I need to know where you all are with numbers. How many of you can add single digit numbers?" A number of hands went up, but some of the youngest children looked doubtful. "How many of you can add two digit numbers together?" Again most of the hands went up. "Three digit numbers?" The hands stayed up.

"All right, how many of you can subtract one number from another?" Again hands went up.

"As long as they are not too big," came a voice.

"If you know the principle, we can work on doing it with any size number," Preacher assured them.

"Now, how many know what multiplication is?" Only a few hands went up. "How about division?" No hands went up.

"I have written some addition problems on the slate. Take your own slates, and work out the answers." Instantly, a babble arose.

"I know, I know. Some of you don't know how to even begin. You who know how to do it, are to help the younger children who don't. I'll give you ten minutes to get done. After that, I'll work out each problem for you, on the slate, and show those of you who are new at it, exactly how to do it step by step. This will be review for most of you, but not for all. Please be patient and show the ones who don't know, how to do it. Go!"

There was a general scramble as the children pulled their slates out from under the benches, and began working on the problems, or looking for someone to help. Preacher sat back in his chair, and watched the stir with interest. It was working! By using the older students to help teach the younger ones, they were feeling important and anxious to show off their knowledge.

The afternoon went quickly, and all too soon it was time to quit for the day. Preacher was almost disappointed. The children were animated and excited after their first real day back at school. It was still snowing lightly as the children trooped out into the late afternoon light.

"Pete, are you sure you are going to be all right?" Preacher called anxiously. "You could stay here for the night, if you want to."

"Naw, I'll be fine! The snow is almost over, and Peachy will get me home just fine. See you tomorrow!" Pete reined the pony around and set off down the trail.

"Well Lord, from my perspective, the first two days were successful. The children seem to have bought into our rules. We got through all of our subjects, I have a pretty good idea of who needs what kind of help, and the children were much better than I was afraid they would be. You came through for me again, and I thank You. The idea of using the older children to help teach the younger ones, worked out just great. Thank You for giving it to me. Now, help me to bring up Your message to them without preaching at them. Please stay with me Lord, I need Your wisdom pretty bad. I know You're always with me, but I thought I'd better tell You, anyway. Amen."

He shrugged into his mackinaw and headed down the hill to Sadie's for his supper.

Chapter 30

The days settled into a routine, with Reading and Writing in the mornings, and Ciphering, Spelling, and sometimes History or Geography in the afternoons. Preacher tried to vary it to keep their attention, and it was going very well. Even Sadie commented on the success of the school, so Preacher knew they were being talked about.

Still, no one showed up for Sunday services, which ate at Preacher. "Lord, I know it's in Your hands. I just need to be faithful, and leave the results to You. But it sure upsets me to see all that is going on in this town, and not being able to feel like I'm influencing anything for You."

The snowstorm had blown away, leaving brilliant blue skies behind. But it was cold for several days, and then the temperature began to warm and the snow to melt. Main Street was in even worse shape, if possible. Now people didn't even try to cross it on the makeshift bridge, but resigned themselves to walking around either end.

Mud was everywhere; mud and half melted ice water. The children were getting cabin fever, so it was a real treat when one day, the snow had melted off the playground enough that Preacher sent the children outside at lunchtime. Pete Tanner was sitting in one of the swings, eating his lunch when Wilbur, one of the bigger boys in school, came up, pushed Pete out of the swing, and sat in it himself.

"You can't do that," Pete shouted. "We have a rule against that."

"Yeah," Wilbur blustered, "and what are you going to do about it, go run to Teacher?"

"I don't need Teacher. I can handle it all by myself!" Pete's face was flushed and his hands balled into fists.

"Just bring it on; you been needin' a good whippin' for a long time. I'm just the one to give it to you," Wilbur stated smugly.

Pete stood seething for a moment, then turned and slowly walked away.

After lunch, Pete was still hot about what Wilbur had done. Wilbur compounded the issue by grinning irritatingly at Pete, whenever he caught his eye. But Pete didn't go tell Preacher about what had happened. Other children carried the tale to him, so he was aware of what was going on. He decided that he wouldn't do anything about it until Pete made a complaint. He would just keep an eye on the situation.

When school was done for the day, the children started gathering up their belongings, and headed out the door to go home. There was Pete, on Peachy, with his ever-present rope in hand and a loop shook-out.

As Wilbur came down the steps of the schoolhouse, Pete swung the loop around his head, and with an easy motion, threw it over Wilbur's shoulders. Peachy, being the good little cow pony she was, immediately backed up, tightening the rope and pulling Wilbur off his feet onto the wet, muddy playground.

Wilbur was livid. He tried to get to his feet, but every time he did, Peachy would back up against the rope and jerk him into the mud again. Wilbur was hollering, cussing, and threatening to do everything and anything to Pete once he got loose. But Pete wasn't letting him loose. Now he nudged Peachy's flanks and the little cow pony begin walking down the trail, dragging Wilbur through the mud, behind her. Wilbur began to scream like a girl, and cry.

Preacher was about to take a hand, when Pete finally shook the rope loose. Wilbur scrambled to his feet, and began running down the trail toward home. But Pete wasn't done. He spurred Peachy after him, and when he got close enough, he popped Wilbur on the butt with the end of that rope. Wilbur would jump and scream and run faster, but Peachy stayed right behind him. Ever so often Pete would pop him again.

Preacher was having a hard time keeping a straight face. He sent the children on their way, and when he was alone, he laughed until his sides hurt. "I guess I won't have to worry about bullying for a while, Lord."

Later, he found out the rest of the story from Sadie. It seems as though Pete ran Wilbur right up to his front door, and then turned to ride home. The door opened, and Wilbur's dad who had a reputation as one of the orneriest lumberjacks in town, came flying out the door yelling and cursing about what had been done to his son, and about what he was going to do about it.

Pete calmly shook out a new loop, and daubed it over the shoulders of the old man. Peachy promptly tightened the rope and jerked the old man off his feet, into the mud -- same routine with the same results. Every time the old man struggled to his feet, Peachy put him back in the mud. Finally, when he saw he wasn't getting anywhere, Wilbur's dad calmed down to a slow boil, and Pete shook off the rope.

"Tell Wilbur if he wants to be a bully, he's got to live with the consequences." Pete reined Peachy around and headed toward home.

Wilbur didn't show up to school for two days. Preacher waited until he had both boys together, to bring up the bullying and fighting rules.

"My inclination is to say that you got as good as you gave Wilbur, and that would be the end of it. But that doesn't address the fact that you both broke the rules we made, and all agreed to. Then, from what I hear, your dad is still pretty mad, Wilbur. I hear he has threatened to whip Pete if he so much as comes near your house, again."

"My dad told him that if he laid a hand on me, he'd get himself whipped by another Tanner," Pete grinned.

"Well that's just dandy! The two of you have started a feud that could get out of hand, if we don't nip it in the bud. Wilbur, you started this whole thing by breaking our no bullying rule. Bullies are cowards who like to throw their weight around when they're bigger, but don't have the sand to stand up when the going is really tough. You don't want the reputation of a bully, Wilbur."

"Pete, instead of coming to me for a solution, you took matters into your own hands. You need to start taming your temper, or it will get you in big trouble later in life. The Bible talks a lot about controlling ourselves. You should come to Sunday meeting and hear what it says."

"Yeah, I guess so," Pete responded.

"All right, here's what is going to happen from here. You two are going to be a pair until further notice. You will sit together, work together, eat together, and help each other. Get the idea? If I call for Pete, Wilbur's ears had better perk up. If I call for Wilbur, Pete had better come running to see what I want." The boys were looking kind of sick.

"Also, the wood box is to be kept full for the next week. So, you will chop wood for an hour after class, all week. Wilbur will chop and Pete will stack for the first half hour, and you will change up for the second half hour. Got it?"

Both boys nodded, but didn't look any too happy with their sentence.

The other children were listening quietly, taking it all in. Preacher turned to everyone. "Our rules are important. You all helped in creating them, and if you don't try to abide by them, that is, if you ignore them, they're just a bunch of words written on a poster board. As you can see, I mean to enforce our rules, and if they're broken, deal out the punishment. Please think about that, as we study together day by day. God deals with us in much the same way. He has given us rules to live our lives by. We haven't done a very good job of living by those rules, so He sent His Son to correct our thinking and provide us the way back into fellowship with God. If you're interested in knowing more about what Jesus said and did for us, I'll be around at recess and after school. You can ask me anything you want to know about it."

There was a general shuffle as the children got out their slates and books for the day.

Chapter 31

The snow continued to melt, so it continued to be muddy and wet. The children were able to go outside for recess, but had to watch where they went to stay out of the mud. Things went along on an even keel, with no more notable incidents, except for the trapping fiasco.

Eddy started it all, because he wanted a new small bore rifle for squirrel hunting. His dad told him that they didn't have money for a new rifle, and if he wanted one he would have to earn his own money to buy it. Well Eddy put his mind to the problem, and came up with an idea. He would trap furs and earn money for the rifle. It seemed like a doable thing, and his dad had some old traps in the barn that he could use for the project.

He planned for days just how and where to do this, and finally the day came when he took the traps out to a likely spot by the creek, and set three of them. He baited them with pieces of an old carcass his dad had discarded, and every morning on his way to school, he would go by to see if he had caught anything. Nothing much happened, except that the old carcass pieces got more and more rank.

One morning, his buddy, Carl showed up at his tent, to walk with Eddy to school. Eddy wanted to check out his traps, so he talked Carl into taking a round-about way to school so he could do so. Nothing was happening at the first trap, so Eddy led the way to the second.

As they got closer, the boys could hear thrashing, hissing and screaming of something. "I got something," Ed crowed, "come on." Indeed he had gotten something, and that something was a skunk which promptly took its pain and anger out on the two boys as soon as they got within range. The boys retreated to a safe distance, but the damage was already apparent. They washed as best they could, in the creek, and went on to school.

At school, Preacher was at the door greeting the children as they arrived, as was his custom. It was a good thing too, because it kept that horrible smell from getting inside the schoolhouse. "You boys go on home. Maybe your mothers will have an idea of how to clean you up. I don't have a clue."

Preacher found out later from Sadie, that the first thing their mothers did was bury their clothes. Then they scrubbed the boys down with lye soap, but it didn't help much. The old Chinese man at the laundry advised that only tomatoes would take away the odor, so every tomato in town was gathered, crushed, and smeared on the boys. Then they were scrubbed down again. It was some better, but not gone by any means.

Another woman said that she heard that lemon juice would take away the smell. Since there were no lemons anywhere around, that didn't help. The women finally decided that they had done about all they could, and the smell would just have to wear off.

Ed's dad didn't really say much. He just shook his head and rode out to shoot the skunk from a safe distance, to put it out of its misery. He told Ed that it would be spring before he could go back to retrieve his trap.

When the boys came back to school, they still smelled pretty bad, so Preacher sat them in the back of the room, as close to the door as possible. Preacher was never sure whether the smell got better, or they all got used to the smell over time. Whatever it was, school went on.

Then one day, it happened. Preacher knew it would, but kept hoping it wouldn't, all the same. Gretchen came to him before school. "Teacher, my ma makes the best tea cake you ever ate. She made one yesterday, and put a piece in my lunch. When I ate my lunch yesterday, it wasn't there, so I asked her when I got home, "Why didn't you put a piece of tea cake in my lunch?" She said, "I did, didn't you get it?" "Teacher, someone is taking things out of our lunches."

Later, one of the boys came to him and said, "Teacher, part of my sandwich was missing when I ate my lunch, and the apple was gone, too." Preacher's heart sank, because he had a suspicion of who it might be.

The next day, Preacher went back to the coat room at recess. He hid behind some coats, in the corner, and watched. Sure enough, a few minutes later a shadow slipped into the coat room, reached up to the shelf where the lunches were kept, and removed a few items from some of them. Then the figure slipped out of the room.

When the children came back in from recess, Preacher stood up in front of the room. "I have had reports of someone taking some items from the lunches left in the coat room. I didn't want to believe it, but I thought I had better check it out. So I hid in the coat room and watched to see what would happen. Sure enough, someone is stealing from the lunches left there. Johnny, would you come up here, please?" The children gasped.

Johnny stood up slowly, his face crimson red. He shook so badly that Preacher wondered if he would be able to walk to the front of the room.

"Johnny, you know what I saw, don't you?" Johnny nodded dumbly. "What did I see?" Preacher tried to ask kindly.

"You saw me taking things out of the other's lunches," Johnny's voice shook.

"That's right, and why did you do that?"

Johnny just stood there, his head down.

Gretchen blurted out, "It's all right, teacher. My mom packs a lot of food for me. It's all right."

"Johnny, why?" Preacher repeated.

"I didn't want to, I was just so hungry. Mom hasn't gotten any washing, and there hasn't been anything to eat for almost two days, now. I'm sorry, I'm really sorry."

"Johnny, it sounds like the other children would have been happy to share their lunches with you, if you had only said something to us."

"Yeah…yeah! I've got plenty. He can have mine," came calls from all around the room.

"I was too ashamed to ask for anything," Johnny confessed.

"Instead, you broke our rule about stealing," Preacher said gently.

"I didn't mean to," Johnny sobbed.

Most of the other children were crying, too. "It's all right, Teacher. He didn't mean it. We forgive him," were some of the cries around the room.

"You know, rules are rules. We can't tailor them to each person or circumstance we encounter. A town or territory or country makes rules for everyone's good. Our rules are the same way. We made them for the good of everyone in our little society of students. If we ignore them for some situations and enforce them for others, that is not fair to all. They soon become worthless or at least subject to influence of the best stories we can tell. Now, yes, Johnny has some special circumstances that caused him to steal, but he didn't *have* to steal. We made a rule because we thought it was important, and we have to enforce that rule. Johnny, you knew the penalty for stealing, but you went ahead and did it anyway."

"Yes sir."

"Well, remove your coat and shirts." It was so quiet, that Preacher could hear the children's breathing, as Johnny slowly began to unpin the old coat around his thin shoulders.

Preacher turned to the slate board and took down the blacksnake whip. It made an angry hiss as he drew it across the floor. When he turned back, Johnny was just pulling the coat open, and Preacher was shocked. It was a cold climate, and all the boys wore sweaters over woolen shirts, with long johns underneath. When Johnny opened his coat, there was nothing but Johnny under it! Preacher took a deep breath when he saw Johnny's thin ribs.

"Bend over the bench, Johnny," Preacher commanded.

"You can't do that Teacher; he can't stand it. It will kill him!" It was Tommy from in back of the room, standing and shouting.

"Yeah, we can't do this," came a chorus of cries.

Preacher held up his hand to silence the children. "I don't want to do this, but it is the penalty we all agreed on at the start of the year. Johnny knew and understood it, too. Any society is only as good as the rules it sets and how well it enforces them. There are always those who, for whatever reason good or bad, break those rules. What we do when it happens tells the world a lot about our society. It tells them how good and just the rules are, others may call them laws. It also tells the world of our resolve in enforcing our rules, so that others who may be tempted to break them may see it and change their minds."

"Yeah, but we didn't know this would happen. We didn't mean for Johnny to go hungry to the point he felt he had to steal to live."

"No, no we did not. In fact it is sympathy and compassion for Johnny's situation that is causing us to have this discussion, right now. I dare say that there isn't one of you who, if Johnny had let you know the situation he is in, would have refused to share with him. The reason he did not let it be known is the old sin of pride. It is embarrassing to him to admit that he needs help. In his life code, to ask for help is a sign of weakness, and he thinks he can fix it himself. In fact, he would rather break our rule, than ask us to help him." Preacher drove home his point by slapping the desk top.

The children jumped and looked down at the floor. They didn't say anything.

Preacher said, "You all are confusing two separate issues. The first is that Johnny and his family needs our help. They are in genuine need. The second is that Johnny broke our rule against stealing, and there is a penalty for having done so. While I don't like it any better than you do, that penalty has to be paid. Johnny, bend over the bench."

Johnny spoke up. "Teacher is right. I did wrong, in spite of knowing better. I deserve the punishment."

Tommy was still adamant. "Teacher, you can't do that, it will kill him. Look at him, all skin and bones, it'll kill him, I tell you."

Preacher looked at the children. "I will be as gentile as I can, he promised."

Johnny bent over the bench and closed his eyes. The girls and more than one of the boys turned their heads.. The whip hissed across the floor.

"Wait"!!! It was Tommy, again. He came striding to the front of the room. "Teacher, you said the penalty has to be paid."

"That's right, Tommy," Preacher replied.

"Well, nothing says who has to pay it." Tommy was belligerent, and his chin jutted out in his passion. "I'm big and strong. Let me take the whippin' for Johnny."

"Well now, I'm not sure…" Preacher was startled.

"Yes, yes, let Tommy do it. He can take it. It won't kill or cripple him. Yes, yes." The children took up the chant.

Preacher held up his hand, and the room became silent. Preacher thought for several seconds, and the children began getting restless.

"No, no it doesn't say anything about who must pay the penalty. We didn't say that the rule-breaker had to pay it, but we all assumed that he or she would be the one. Is this what you all want?" Preacher asked.

"Yes… yes," all the children cried. "Tommy can do it. He's big and strong. Show him, Tommy."

Tommy peeled off his thick sweater, unbuttoned his wool shirt, unbuttoned his long johns down to his waist, and peeled the top down. "All right, Teacher, I'm ready."

Tommy was indeed an imposing figure next to Johnny.

Johnny said, "You don't have to do this, Tommy. I'm the one who stole."

Tommy nodded at the younger boy. "Just stand back, I'll take care of it."

Tommy bent over the bench. "All right, Teacher. Let's get it over with."

Preacher nodded, and brought the whip down as gently as he could, across Tommy's back. Tommy winced and bit his lip.

"One."

Preacher adjusted his stance. The whip hissed across the floor.

"Two." the children took up the count.

Tommy's face screwed up in pain, but he didn't make a sound. Preacher shook his head. *I can't do this*, he thought.

"Three, four, five."

Now Tommy's tears were staining the plank floor. He groaned as the whip bit his back, again.

"Six."

Now, there wasn't a dry eye in the school house.

"Seven, eight."

Johnny knelt at his head and wiped the sweat from Tommy's face.

"Nine."

Tommy cried out hoarsely. Then mercifully, it was done.

"Ten."

Tommy rolled off the bench in a dead faint, but his head never hit the floor. Johnny was there, cradling his head in his lap, his tears washing Tommy's face.

"Oh, Tommy… Tommy. No one has ever done something like this for me. I'll be your friend forever. Anything you ever need, I'm your friend." And he gently rocked Tommy's head as he cried.

"Get the liniment," Preacher commanded.

Gretchen ran to find it.

By the time she got back, Tommy's eyes were open and he was looking around in confusion at all the stir. Preacher sat him up and began to apply the liniment to the stripes.

"You're going to be sore for a few days, but you'll be all right, and this liniment should help," Preacher commented. "Now, everyone sit down, I have a few things I need to say to you all."

The children all split up, their excitement over but not forgotten. As they took their seats, to get settled, Preacher began to speak.

"What we have just witnessed... what Tommy did, was a courageous and noble thing. The Bible says, 'Greater love hath no man, than that he lay down his life for his friend'."

"But it was not the first time someone has willingly paid the penalty for another's sin. As this incident unfolded, my spirit was crying out to God, why? Why now? Why this? Our school year was going so well. You all have been learning a lot, participating and helping each other. From my perspective, we have been having a good time together. Why did God allow something like this to happen? Then it came to me. As you all know, I came to town hoping to spread the Gospel of Jesus Christ in this area. I was talked into filling the need for a school master until another can be found. Don't get me wrong, I love what I'm doing, and I love each of you. But, I keep praying that God will allow me to spread His Gospel of grace."

"I prayed for that again this morning, before school started. And God has answered my prayer. What a beautiful illustration of what Jesus did for each of us on the cross. He, God's only begotten Son, Who never sinned, willingly laid down His life to pay the just penalty for our sin, demanded by God's justice as payment when sin entered the world."

"Just as Tommy willingly put his life up for Johnny's sin of stealing, Jesus knowing we could not live paying our own penalty offered His life in our place. The difference is that while Tommy was beaten, Jesus was beaten, cursed, then nailed to a cross and killed to pay the price of our sin. His death satisfied the death penalty that all of mankind is under, and God looks at us just as if we had never sinned. That is called justification. All we have to do is do for Him is what Johnnie did for Tommy. Recognize the great gift Jesus has given us, and trust that what He did for us on the cross does what He has promised it would do; that is, makes us right with God the Father. It's a free gift, and all we have to do is accept it. But we each have to accept His free gift for ourselves. It's like I hold out a gift for you, but it's not yours, until you take it."

"You can do that right now, right there on the bench you're sitting on. You just say to Him in your heart, "I know I'm a sinner. I know Jesus came to pay the penalty for my sin. I know He is the Son of God, and that He came to earth, lived a sinless life, and died on the cross for me. I accept the free gift of eternal life He offers, and ask Him to be my Savior." The Bible says, 'But to as many as received Him, to them He gave the right to be called the children of God.' So on His authority, if you prayed that prayer and meant it in your heart of hearts, you are God's child. The Bible also says, 'He who confesses Me before men, the same will I confess before My Father in heaven.' So it's important for you to tell your folks and others of your new commitment. You can also tell me, and I will pray for you and try to help you in your new faith, however I can."

"I prayed that prayer, Teacher... Preacher"

"Yeah, me too."

"Yeah, yeah, yeah." came voices all around.

"Great! That's great. I think I'll dismiss school for the day. It's Friday afternoon, and I have to think about what I can do to help Johnny and his family."

Preacher looked over at Johnny who still had red eyes which he kept wiping every now and again.

"We want to help, too," came a chorus of voices. "I know my dad will help when he hears what happened. Yeah... yeah."

"Tommy, how are you doing?" Preacher looked over at the boy sitting on the bench with several of the girls clustered around him

"It hurts when I move much, but I'm all right. Count me in, I want to help, too."

"All right, how about this? You all go home now, and talk to your folks. Whatever you decide to do, you can bring it back to the school house. I should think flour, corn meal, bacon, ham, things like that will keep, and should last a while. We'll meet here at 10:00 tomorrow if you can, and take whatever we have over to Johnny's place. In the meantime, I'll have Sadie send over food for tonight.

"That's a good plan." The children got to their feet and headed toward the door.

"Goodbye, see you, tomorrow," Preacher called out.

"I think I'll just sit here for a while, and then I think I can get home," Tommy said.

"I'll stay with you, and then help you get home," Johnny promised. Preacher smiled. Johnny was anxious to do whatever he could do for Tommy. He'd stay there all night if need be.

"I'm going to make arrangements with Sadie. Will you boys be all right here, until I get back?"

"We'll be fine, Teacher." Tommy replied. "I'm just going to sit here and let the liniment work on the burn in my back. Could I have some water, please?"

Johnny jumped up. "I'll get it," and he scampered off.

"My dad doesn't have much truck with religion." Tommy said. "I prayed that prayer, and I'll tell him. When I do, I may get another beatin'."

"I sincerely hope not, Tommy. Would you like me to be with you when you tell him?"

"No, it'll be all right. I'll just make sure he's sober when I tell him."

"Well Tommy, this is the most important decision you'll ever make. And God's Holy Spirit is with you every step along the path of life, to strengthen, help, and comfort you when things do get tough," Preacher explained.

"I know I feel different," Tommy said. "I can't explain it, but I just feel clean."

"I know, I remember the feeling. Just don't depend on the feeling. It will wear off, but God has promised, and He never goes back on His Word. It's sort of like getting a new saddle. Remember how good it smells when you carry it out of the store?"

Tommy nodded.

"Well, before long that new leather and oil smell fades away, but you still have the saddle. It still does the same thing it did when it was new, you can still touch it and see it on the saddle-tree. Well, that's the way it is with God. The newness will wear off eventually, because we're only men. But God is still there. He never changes, never goes back on His word."

Johnny came back with the water.

"Thanks little buddy." Tommy said gratefully, and took a long drink.

"I *am* your buddy, you know, Johnny said.

"I do know." Tommy reached out and squeezed Johnny's arm.

Preacher nodded. "I'm going to see Sadie, now. I'll be back in a little while. You two just stay around here until I get back. Help yourself to whatever you need. I'll be back, soon. He went out the door.

When he came back, Tommy was feeling a little better.

"I think I can get home, now."

"I'll go with him," Johnny chimed in.

154

"I'll come with you, and tell your father what happened," Preacher said.

"No, it'll be all right; maybe better if I explain things myself," Tommy insisted.

Tommy winced as he tried to put his shirt on. "I think I'll just go home like this," he decided.

"If your dad wants to talk to me about any of this, I'll be right here," Preacher promised.

The boys went out the door together.

Chapter 32

Saturday, before 10:00 am the school yard began to fill up with buggies and wagons. It seemed that everyone had heard of what had happened at school the day before, and the need of one of their own families. Preacher got excited as he saw the community pulling together to meet the need. Even the mayor was there, sober for once. *Maybe it is too early in the day, even for him*, Preacher thought.

Preacher began to address the crowd, as even as more wagons were pulling up.

"Friends, this is great! You all know why we are here, and I have two mixed thoughts about how we should proceed. One is that it would be good for Johnny's family to know how much we all esteem them, and wish to help in this time of want. They need to know they're not in this alone. But I feel that some of you would prefer that your help be anonymous. Please tell me what you want to do. How many would like to take your gift to Johnny's family, yourself?"

Several hands sent up.

"How many wish to remain anonymous?"

Other hands went up.

Preacher thought a minute. "All right, here's what we're going to do. Those who wish to remain anonymous will leave their gifts in the school house. The rest of us will load up whatever wagons are left and carry all the gifts to the Jamison family. Mr. Mayor, will you be our spokesman?"

"Hmm, why, of course. It's my duty. Be glad to help!"

"Thank you. Let's get started," Preacher instructed.

The pile of goods grew rapidly. True to his suggestions, Preacher saw a slab of beacon, two hams, flour, corn meal, pinto beans, and more. One enterprising family brought six chickens in a crate. Another had a nanny-goat on a rope tied to their wagon. These were good, caring people, and Preacher's heart was drawn to them in a way it had not been up until then. The people kept coming and bringing food, until Preacher thought it would never end.

Finally, a man came up with nothing in his hands.

"My name is Harvey Burke. I'm the owner of the Mercantile in town."

"I know who you are, Mr. Burke." Preacher answered. "You and your wife displayed my church notice, when I first came into town."

"Well, I was thinking about what I could contribute to the cause. I wanted whatever I did to last for more than a few weeks, so I finally hit on an idea. I know Mr. Jamison has been hurt, and can't do much. But he could maybe sweep out my store, and watch things when I have to step out. If he is willing, I'll hire him. I can't pay him much, but it will give him something to occupy his time, and a little money to help." Mr. Burkes' voice trailed off.

Preacher grabbed his hand and pumped it vigorously. "That may be the best medicine he could get, Mr. Burke."

"Come on, men, let's load this all up and get it to where it's needed," Preacher directed.

The men set to with a will, and soon all the goods were loaded onto wagons and the party set off for the Jamison tent.

As they approached the tent, Johnny came out, followed by his father on makeshift crutches, his mother drying her hands on her apron, and two pre-school aged youngsters. Mrs. Jamison came running when she saw it was Preacher. She threw her arms around his neck, and hugged until Preacher thought she would squeeze his head off. "Oh, thank you, thank you, thank you. That was the first good meal we've had in forever. The little ones went to bed without crying with hunger for the first time in a long time. You're truly an angel."

Preacher pulled away from her. "That's the second time I've been called an angel. I'm no angel, just a man who tries to do what God asks him to do. I'm no different from these other folks," he waved his hand the other people with him. "God moved their hearts to help, too."

The mayor moved forward. "Mrs. Jamison, family, as Mayor of the fine city of West Fork, it is my pleasure to present to you, the solicitations of your friends and neighbors, many of whom wish to remain anonymous. What you see in these wagons comes with our sincere good wishes for a speedy recovery."

Mrs. Jamison was overcome. She hid her face in her apron and cried, her body shaking with emotion. Jamison himself was pale with shock. "I didn't think anybody knew or cared," he muttered.

Johnny jumped around in excitement. "I told you, I told you," he kept shouting.

"Come on," Preacher called, "let's get this unloaded. The chickens will have to stay in the crate until you get a pen built," Preacher said to Johnny. He nodded.

"Tie the goat to that old stump over there. She's in season, so the youngsters should get plenty of milk," said a man leading the goat.

Soon, the things were all unloaded, and the townsfolk climbed up into the wagons and prepared to disperse. Harvey Burke stepped forward. "John, I need some help at the store. I know you can't do much, but you can be my eyes and ears. You can sweep up at your own pace. It's not much, but it will keep you busy, and give you a bit of coin to jingle in your pockets. If you're interested, be at the Emporium Monday morning. I'll show you what to do."

Tears sprang into John Jamison's eyes, and he turned away quickly. "I'll be there," he said hoarsely.

Preacher smiled and sighed. *More than we ask or think Lord*, he thought.

Chapter 33

Sunday dawned grey and overcast. Preacher opened the school house doors early, as usual, and stood on the step as he had done every Sunday since he had been there. His heart was heavy. Yes, it was true that yesterday had exceeded all of his hopes. Jamisons would be all right now, he knew. But this was Sunday. He was doing what he had done for many weeks, and no one, not a one had shown any interest in God or spiritual things. He had little hope that today would be any different.

"What are You trying to show me, Lord?" he prayed.

Then, around the corner of the building came the Jamison family. All of them, in the best, cleanest clothes they had.

"At least, it's something Lord," the smiled broadly. "Welcome," he called.

Then he heard the sound of wheels, and one of the wagons that had been there yesterday, was back. This time it was filled with one of the lumberjack's family. Preacher's heart leaped. *Could it be? Could the Lord be using the plight of one family to stir the hearts of this community? Could this be the start of what he had earnestly prayed for, since he first came into town? That's it, Lord. You're showing me that I can plant and water, but You give the increase, in Your time.*

Other buggies and wagons were arriving.

"Lord, it's a miracle," Preacher breathed.

Preacher greeted each one as they filed into the school house. When they quit coming, there were twenty-two seated on the benches, greeting each other and talking among themselves.

Preacher took up his banjo, strummed a few bars to get their attention.

"Stand up with me and praise our great God as we sing Rock of Ages, cleft for me."

Some didn't know all the words, but their fervor made up for it.

Once they had sat back down, Preacher welcomed them.

"My text for this morning comes from Luke 15, verses 11 through 31."

Preacher began to read the account of the prodigal son. There was some squirming as Preacher read. When he finished, he looked over the group that had assembled.

"Some of you are like that prodigal son. You have wandered far away. Perhaps you were taught about God's goodness at your mother's knee. Perhaps, she prayed for you, perhaps she sang the old hymn we just sang. Perhaps, your father prayed asking God to bless his efforts to provide for you and the rest of the family. Perhaps, he loaded the family into the wagon and took you to Sunday services, perhaps not. Whatever, the case, you have decided to gather today to pay your respects to God. And He is worthy of our respect, of our awe, of our devotion."

"This parable or story Jesus used to drive home his point shows us something of the character of our Father in heaven.

He waits patiently for us, anxiously looking for us to come back to Him. You see, he owns us because He made us. But we have decided that the grass looks better in that far country. We stubbornly go off to see what it is like. Then when we get ourselves in over our heads, we remember how good we had it back with Dad."

"The good news is that our Father is still waiting for us. He hasn't moved, He hasn't given up on us, He hasn't forgotten us. When we decide that we're tired of the slop the world feeds us, and turn to go back to Him, He runs to meet us. Not to just hold us down like bugs and watch us squirm, but he restores us to the position we enjoyed when He first made us, and declares us righteous, just like we had never run off like that in the first place."

"You all know what happened here at school, this past week. It is something I never anticipated, did not want, and wished would go away, at the time. We had a student step in for another and pay a penalty that he didn't deserve, for the one who couldn't pay the price of his misdeed, himself. It is a picture of what Jesus, God's only begotten Son has done for us. He has paid a penalty that would kill us, so that we might live. All we have to do is turn around and go to the Father, Who is waiting with his hands outstretched in love."

"God has used what I thought was totally negative, a disaster really, to perform a miracle in this community. You've taken the first step back to Him. He welcomes you back. Won't you complete the trip back? He'll welcome you right now. Bow your heads with me."

Preacher led them through the sinner's prayer.

"If any of you have prayed that prayer, please lift your hand. I want to pray for you this week, and the decision you have made." No one stirred. *Well, Lord I planted and watered, it's up to You now.* Preacher thought.

As he stood at the door, several folks had positive comments to make. "We'll be back next Sunday, Preacher." said one man. Mr. Latimer stopped by with his wife at his side. "Preacher, I fried up a chicken for dinner today. Would you join my husband and me for lunch?" Mrs. Latimer asked.

"My dear lady, I would be delighted," Preacher responded. "Just let me bid farewell to the rest of these folks, and I'll be ready.

"Impressive service, Preacher."

"Well said."

"Gave us something to think about."

Finally, the last of them exited the school house and headed home. Preacher turned to the Latimers. "I think I'm ready," he said.

"Come on then, our buggy is over here." Latimer said.

Mrs. Latimer was a good cook and Preacher was thoroughly enjoying himself. A piece of peach pie after the fried chicken, potatoes, gravy, and pinto beans, had Preacher pondering the joys of domestic life, when Latimer cleared his throat, and launched into the reason for the lunch invitation.

"In your address, you painted a picture of God as a loving Father waiting anxiously for the return of His wayward son."

"I would hasten to point out that Jesus spoke the parable, and it is a glimpse into God's character," Preacher responded.

"Yes, yes, I will concede that for most people, but what if God has turned His back on someone? Does it mean that they area forever outside of God's mercy?"

So, this was the reason he had been invited here. Preacher looked down at his plate considering his response. He had the sense that if Latimer felt he was getting a glib answer, he would dismiss it and the opportunity would be lost.

"That is a very interesting question, Mr. Latimer. And it has a somewhat complicated answer," Preacher began. "Do you feel that God has turned His back on you?"

Latimer squirmed in his chair and looked uncomfortable, but to his credit, he met Preacher's eye, and responded, "It has crossed my mind, with the kind of life I've lived."

"Ask any man on the hill, and they'll tell you that I am the best jack around. I lay more sticks on the ground than any two other men. I work hard, and when I'm done, I play hard. I don't make excuses and I don't accept them, either."

"Mrs. Latimer is not your wife, is she?" Preacher spoke low, but clearly.

Latimer looked embarrassed. "Her husband was killed on the hill, last year. He was a fool. He was bucking for a promotion to foreman, and cutting corners to keep his production up and look good for the boss, when he miscalculated. A log he was cutting bucked back, like they will sometimes do. He wasn't watching, and the butt caught him between it and another log. Smashed him like a bug."

"As a single man, I had been watching Mary for some time. She's a fine-looking piece… er… woman. Now she was alone, with no one to help her, no place to go, so I moved in on the situation. Told her she and the twins could move in with me. I would take care of them… if she would take care of me."

"I ain't no saint, but she would have starved and the kids too, if I hadn't done what I did. I've been pretty good to them, but I like to lift a few with the other guys, after the work week, and I guess I've been a little mean when I'm liquored up. Now she says that if I slap her or the twins around again, she'll leave me or kill me one." The last was stated in an 'in your face' take it or leave it attitude.

Preacher leaned back in his chair. "I'm not here to judge you, Mr. Latimer. That's God's job. I don't have all the answers and never have had. You work for a boss, so you know what I mean when I tell you that I do too. I just try to do what He tells me to do, when He tells me to do it. I can tell you what His Word says."

"So, tell me. That's what I want."

"The Bible says that His, that is God's, Spirit will not always strive with our spirit. It goes on to say, 'Behold now is the accepted time. Behold, today is the day of salvation.' So, apparently, there can come a time when God's Holy Spirit can quit trying to get our attention, quit trying to lead us back home as I talked about in my sermon."

"We don't know when that point is. It may be different for different people. We do know that the thief, who was executed on the cross next to Jesus, was accepted when he turned in faith to Him. Jesus told him, "Today, thou shalt be with me in paradise." So that shows us that it is never too late."

"The Word also says that, 'He who cometh to me, I will in no wise cast out.' That is a flat promise with no time limit or conditions. We just need to come to Jesus as we are. Your invitation to me today and your questions, show me that it is not too late for you. God is still working in your life, drawing you to Himself. The time is not past. He wants you to come to Him. It is His job to change your attitude about some of these situations you have told me about today. I will caution you, however. We don't know when the time comes that God's Holy Spirit will not work on us any more. If that happens, it *is* too late. Don't you want to settle it right now?"

"Oh, John, don't say no. This is a chance for us. I know it is." It was Mary, who had been listening quietly to all that had been said. She was crying freely as she knelt by Latimer's chair.

"What do I have to do?" Latimer asked hoarsely.

"God knows your heart, so you just tell Him what you want. I'll help you with a prayer to Him, if you want."

"All right."

"Just repeat after me, you too, Mary. Jesus, I am coming to you as a sinner. I have tried to clean myself up many times, but I just can't do it. I need You. I know that God sent You to die for my sins, and I thank You that You were willing to do it. I accept Your free gift and ask You to blot out my sins. Make me a new creation, as Your Word promises. Amen."

"According to His Word, you are now children of God. In the first chapter of John, and in verses 11 and 12 we're told, 'He came unto his own, but His own received Him not. But unto as many as received Him to them gave He the right to be called children of God'."

"That's it? It was that easy? Are you sure?" Latimer was excited, now.

"God knows your heart. He knows if you really meant that prayer. Based on His Word, if you prayed that prayer, in faith believing, you are His child."

"I do feel light, like I'm really alive," Latimer said.

"Me, too," Mary was giggling like a schoolgirl.

"Don't depend on that feeling, it may fade over time. Depend on God's promise. It never changes, and He has promised that 'He who cometh to me, I will in no wise cast out'."

"You need to begin reading the Bible regularly. It will tell you everything you need to know. Do you have a Bible?"

Latimer frowned. "No, I never had use for that."

But Mary's eyes lit up. "I have my mother's Bible in my trunk. I'll get it."

"I'm not much for reading, Preacher. Never learned how very good."

"That's all right, John. I'm out of practice, but I think I can still do it, and I'll read to you," Mary said gaily.

"That'll work," John agreed.

"A good place to start is the book of John, in the new testament. You'll have questions, and you can always ask me. I'll do anything I can do to help you."

"Well then, you can start off by marrying us, legal like. Wouldn't look right to continue living in sin, now would it?" Latimer asked.

"I'll be right happy to oblige you, Mr. Latimer. You know God created marriage, and we're always better off doing things His way."

"Mary, call in the kids, might as well do it right now, and call me John," Latimer boomed.

Mary flushed.

"All right, John. May I suggest something for your consideration?" Preacher asked.

John nodded.

"It may be more meaningful to Mary, if your friends and neighbors could witness your marriage. That way it's clear to everyone, and leaves nothing for gossips to talk about," Preacher suggested.

"Please, John. That would be grand," Mary breathed.

"I don't care what gossips say, but if that's what you want…" John relented.

Mary nodded.

"I'll tell Hiz'onor the mayor, and he can pass the word. We'll do it next Sunday after church," Latimer decided.

"We can do it right there in the school house, if you wish," Preacher suggested.

"Fine, fine," Latimer grinned. He just wanted to tie up a few loose ends and he didn't care about the details.

They talked a little longer about various things, but it was clear to Preacher that the issue he had been invited to address, had been taken care of. After a short time, Preacher took his leave. "That was as fine a meal as I have ever had," Preacher bowed low over Mary's hand.

Mary blushed, and said they would do it again, soon.

Then Preacher walked back to the school house.

Chapter 34

The next day at school was a whirlwind for Preacher. The children were excited and clamoring, so that he had trouble getting them settled down enough to start their lessons.

"My parents say that you're a good preacher."

"Yeah, mine say they plan to go back every Sunday."

"My mom cried all afternoon, she was so happy that she got my dad to go."

"My mom and daddy-to-be are getting married!" This last was shouted over the hubbub, and the room became instantly quiet.

Preacher said, "That's right. It will happen next Sunday, right after the morning service."

"Preacher, er... Teacher, what do we call you now, anyway?"

Preacher laughed. "I think Mr. Scott or Teacher is still appropriate. I haven't changed; I'm still the same man I was on Friday."

"Speaking as Teacher, get out your readers, and open them to where we left off on Friday. Ida, I think it was your turn next, when we left off."

There was a general stir as the children got out their McGuffy readers.

"All right Ida, begin reading at the second paragraph."

As she began the exercise, Preacher's mind began to wander. So much had happened, just overnight, it seemed. Where he had seen no apparent progress getting his church ministry going, overnight it seemed to have blossomed. Where he had been discouraged and disheartened, he now saw endless possibilities, and was excited beyond anything he had experienced. The joy of seeing God's truth taking root and beginning to bear fruit in that place, made him almost shout aloud.

"Thank You, Lord," he breathed. "It has all been worth it."

He suddenly realized that Ida had quit reading, and the class was looking expectantly at him. He cleared his throat, and said. "Thank you Ida."

"Well was that right?" she asked indignantly. "Co-log-ne? I've never heard of it, before."

"It is a French word, pronounced cologne, Ida. It is a scent sometimes used by European women to make themselves smell good."

"My mom uses lilac water, sometimes."

"Yes, that's the same idea," Preacher smiled. *Guess I'd better keep my mind on what I'm supposed to be doing,* Preacher thought, *or I might be giving the right answer to the wrong question.*

The rest of the day passed uneventfully in spite of stray thoughts, memories, plans, and the excitement of the success he had caught a glimpse of.

Almost before he knew it, Preacher was saying, "Good job today class, see you tomorrow," and the children were trouping out the door to go home.

Preacher headed down the hill to get his supper at Sadies, and found that his day at school was only the tip of the iceberg. The whole town was alive with the buzz of what had happened on Sunday.

"D*@#est thing I ever seen. He's not the same guy who drank me under the table on Friday."

"Got religion, they say…."

"Marriage on Sunday? What's he need to buy the cow for? He already is getting all the milk he wants… haw, haw, haw."

"First congregation since…"

"Fool to think these lumberjacks…"

The conversation boiled and swirled like a witch's cauldron. Everyone had an opinion, and felt free to express it.

"Evening, Preacher."

"Hello, Reverend."

"Is it true?"

Preacher sat at his table and felt it all churning around him. *Lord, when You act, You really let it go, don't You? I don't think I have ever heard such a unified topic of conversation. I couldn't even get a grunt in response to 'God bless you.' and now all I'm hearing is about what happened this last weekend. Thank You, Lord, for Your faithfulness. You have promised that if You be lifted up, You will draw all men to Yourself. Help me to proclaim Your Word faithfully. Amen.*

Then someone slipped into the chair opposite Preacher. "Hello, Preacher, didn't think to see me tonight, did you?"

Preacher looked into the eyes of the sheriff. "Hello, Sheriff. What brings you here this time of night? Thought you would be busy at Grady's, by now."

"Oh, I'm on duty, all right. But I knew you would be coming down for your supper, so I've been watching for you."

"For me? Whatever for?" He had Preacher's full attention, now.

"Well, for a couple of reasons. First is, I was wrong about you. I had you pegged for some mealy-mouthed psalm-singer who wouldn't last as long as it took me to get rid of you. I figured sending you to the tender mercies of 'Hiz'onor' would cause you to cave in, turn tail and run. But what I found out is that you've got more sand than the mayor and the rest of the town combined. I was wrong, and when I'm wrong, I'm man enough to own up to it!"

"Well, thanks, Sheriff, but you have nothing to 'own up' to. It's all been God's doing. He is faithful, and big enough to get any job done He wants to do. All I had to do is obey when He showed me what I should do."

"Yeah... all right. However you want to cut it, all I know is that I have to admire you, and congratulate you on the job you have done with the children. Now, you're starting to stir up the townsfolk, too. They're beginning to sit up and take notice. I never thought you had a chance..." The sheriff shook his head in disbelief.

"God is in control, Sheriff. I lost sight of that myself for a little while, and got discouraged. But He got me back on track, and now I believe that more than ever. This is a good town with good people in it. If God is given His rightful place here, it could be a great town." Preacher warmed up to his topic.

"Well, I now know better than to bet against you and God," the sheriff stated positively.

"The other reason I looked you up tonight, is that a rider came in this afternoon with a messages from Sheriff Micah Tate. Know 'im?"

Preacher nodded. "Sheriff in Haskell," he said.

"That's him. Seems that he wanted to get a message to both of us. He says that The Brotherhood, whatever that is, is spreading across the mountain, this way. Now, I have to go back over to Grady's. Been away too long as it is, so I don't have time for long explanations right now. But tomorrow, can you swing by my office and fill me in on what is going on, and who or what this Brotherhood is?"

"I can do it after school hours, Sheriff."

"All right, about 3:30, 4:00?" asked the sheriff, wanting something definite.

"Fine, see you, then," Preacher replied.

Chapter 35

The next day, Preacher dismissed class at 3:15, pulled the door closed, and headed down the hill to the sheriff's office. As he opened the door, the sheriff was just pouring coffee in two cups from a pot on the wood stove.

"Good timin'," the sheriff said. "I had Sadie deliver a pot of joe for us to talk around. From the look on your face when I mentioned the Brotherhood last night, you got a story to tell."

"Yes, and it's one I thought I'd left behind, but it seems they have other plans. I hate to bring it up, but as they say 'to be forewarned is to be forearmed', so I'd better bring you up to date." Preacher took the offered cup, and sat down in the other chair.

"It all started on the trail into Haskell." Preacher continued, recounting his meeting of Elizabeth Strong; of helping her get away from the Brotherhood; of Jeremy Maxwell coming to Haskell; of his beating and long recovery; of bearding the Brotherhood over the issue of the trunk; of the marriage between Elizabeth and Jeremy, and their leaving for Ohio.

"Now, I'm beginning to wonder if they really got away all right," Preacher mused.

"Well the sheriff in Cedar City is a friend of mine, so I'll send an inquiry his way. We'll find out for sure." The sheriff refilled the coffee cups.

"When I was sure they were on their way, I came to West Fork to start the work here. Sheriff Tate rode out to the trail fork with me, which at the time I thought was a mite overcautious on his part, but now… Then I heard that person prowling around after I'd made camp. When I hailed him, he wouldn't come in or even answer me. The next day, I saw his boot tracks, so I know someone was there."

"Skedaddled, huh?"

"Evidently, when he knew I was still up and alert, he headed out fast."

"You're lucky you weren't bushwhacked."

"Maybe, but God is in control, and He knew He wanted me in West Fork."

The sheriff threw back his head and guffawed. "And I thought you were nuts, that day when you came in here. I knew everyone would be against you from the start. You were spitting into the wind, Preacher."

Preacher nodded. "I got that idea. But you didn't count on God. All he needs is for us to do what He asks us to do. He'll do the rest."

Sheriff sobered. "This Brotherhood sounds like a bad outfit. Sounds like this Eli Thomas plays the tune and the rest dance the jig."

"What I can't figure is why they are coming this way. It can't be that they are just after me, although I'm sure they wouldn't miss a chance to do me harm if they could. But they didn't know where I was going or what I was doing." Preacher scratched his head.

"Well, it may explain what has been happening back up the valley toward the pass," Sheriff said thoughtfully. "Miz Downey, Rose Downey, lives up that way with her granddaughter. Jud Downey died three, maybe four years ago. She's been running the ranch with her granddaughter and some hired hands, ever since. She's tough! Capable as most men, maybe more than some, but she's had trouble over the last several months with someone running off her cattle, shooting some, rerouting her water. Being the only law in the area, she comes in to me for help, even though she lives way outside my jurisdiction. Maybe this Brotherhood is causing her problems."

"Possible, but it's not the kind of activity we saw in Haskell. They weren't openly breaking the law, there."

"You're right. Something definitely has gotten their attention in this area of the country, but what is it?" the sheriff pondered.

"Well, one thing is sure. We both need to keep our eyes and ears open. Get word to me about anything you learn, and I'll do the same. You'd better start packing a gun. Do you even have one or know how to shoot one?" the sheriff asked speculatively.

"No, I don't carry one, and have no intention of starting. God has taken care of me for over thirty years, and I see no reason He needs my help, now."

"Suit yourself, but I know from experience, if someone starts shooting at you, you'll feel pretty naked without one," the sheriff countered.

Preacher rose to go. "I'll be down at Sadie's getting my supper. If you need anything more, you can find me there."

"Fair enough… I can't think of anything more, right now."

"See ya'."

"Yup."

Preacher wandered down the backside of the tents and few buildings to where Sadie, sweating profusely and wiping damp curls out of her eyes, was serving an overflow crowd at the diner. "I think there's a place over there, Preacher. Just find what you can, and I'll be with you, directly. One more special, Mac," she yelled at the cook.

Preacher edged around the room and finally spotted an empty chair next to a strapping lumberjack whose shaved head was a source of pride, in spite of the cold weather. In fact, it had caused more than one fight when someone saw fit to rib him about it.

"Hello, Curly. Mind if I sit down?" Preacher grinned.

"Help yourself, Preacher. I'm about done, so I won't be much company, but if you don't mind that, I don't."

"Didn't see you at the service. Wish you would come by and give it a try."

"Well, no offense, Preacher, but I got no truck with religion. The only religion I got is these." He held up two ham-sized hands. "They usually keep me pretty straight with people," he added.

Preacher chuckled. "I'm sure they straighten people right up."

Curly grinned right back, but didn't deny it.

"Any news out in the woods these days?" Preacher was just killing time, waiting for Sadie to come by.

"Naw, just some deer and a 'coon now and again. Nothin' to talk about. But come to think about it, there was some kind of surveyor and his helper... strange little guy." Curly shook his head. "Something about looking for a route for a railroad, or something. They kind of stay out of sight so as not to get people riled up. But I saw them and talked to them, so they's around."

"Probably don't want to stir up land speculators with rumors," Preacher reasoned. All the time he was thinking, *I've got to see the sheriff, again.*

"Yeah, well I'm done and I want to get on down to Grady's. There's a poker game I want to get in on. See you, around, Preacher."

Sadie ambled up alongside the table and set the 'special' in front of Preacher. "Here ya' go, hon'. Buffaler steak, greens, and grits. Coffee in the jug, and I'll bring your favorite apple pie, later."

Preacher suddenly had an appetite. He had news for the sheriff.

Chapter 36

Then he heard it, the clang of the fire bell! People jumped up and began running. Men were shouting, women screaming. Shouts for buckets and water could be heard everywhere.

When Preacher got outside, he could see an orange glow on the east end of town.

"We got to hurry; or it could take the whole town!"

"Thank God there is no wind, tonight!"

"Bring those buckets. Here, give me one!"

It was chaos! Preacher was swept along with the throng.

"It's Lars Pederson's tent. Wasn't he just in Grady's, celebrating his birthday?"

The bucket brigade was forming fast, and Preacher joined in. Bucket after bucket came down the line, as fast as hands could pass them. But everyone knew it was too late. It quickly became an effort to keep the neighboring tents from catching. Preacher's back soon began to ache and his arms began to tremble with fatigue. Still the buckets came. He was about to go to his knees, when an arm went around his waist, and a voice said, "Come on, Preacher. You're needed over here."

Preacher looked up into the face of Curly.

"Come on."

Preacher stumbled along after Curly to the smoldering remains of the original tent. There he saw Lars Pedersen, huddled on the ground, crying and moaning incoherently. There also were three bodies laid out on the ground; two little ones, babies, really, and what was obviously Lars' wife.

"She couldn't get them out, she couldn't get them out," Lars moaned over and over.

Those standing nearby shook their heads in sorrow, and helplessness at his grief.

"Can you do something? We don't know what to do," Curly whispered. "He's my best friend, and I can't help him."

Preacher sank to his knees beside Lars, cradled his big blond head in his arms, raised his face to heaven, and began to pray.

"Almighty God, Creator and Sustainer of life, Comforter and Strong Rock, we need You this very moment. We need Your sweet Comfort and Your tender care, because we have nothing else to cling to. We claim Your promise that if we cry out to You, You will hear us and answer our need. Three have been taken from our midst. We will no longer enjoy their fellowship, nor will we hear their laughter and song. They are in Your presence. You, Who love them far more and more perfectly than our poor efforts ever could. We trust them to Your care and ask for Lars to feel the comfort that only You can provide. Amen."

As he prayed, Preacher could feel Lars' body gradually relaxing.

"Run and see if the company doctor will give you some laudanum for him," Preacher directed.

"Why did this happen?" someone asked.

"Now, maybe you will listen to me when I tell you we have to get rid of these tents, and build more permanent buildings." It was the mayor, and he was seizing the moment to push his agenda.

"Now mayor, we've been over this before, and now is not the time."

"No? Well when will be the time?" Hiz'oner was red faced with passion. "This should not have happened!"

"It's my fault." Lars, face in his hands, was speaking slowly, dully. "It 's my birthday. Normally, I don't really even notice it, but my friends on the crew found out about it and decided to take me out for a drink at Grady's. I don't really drink, so it didn't take much for me to feel it. Next thing I knew, I was in my tent. Dori had left a candle for me to see by. I was befuddled and clumsy, and I knocked it over into a pile of clothes. I tried to put it out, and throw the pile outside, but I just scattered it. By the time Dori woke up and saw what was happening, the whole tent was ablaze. And now... oh God, oh God!"

Lars began rocking and moaning again.

"Is here someone in town who can build us some coffins?" Preacher asked.

"The Mercantile carries one or two in case of emergencies. They can probably help us."

"All right, we'll hold a service at the school house at 10:00 in the morning. We will need to get them taken care of right away," Preacher said. "Is there a town cemetery, yet?"

"Yeah, about a mile out west of town."

"We'll need a couple of gravediggers in the morning."

"I know a couple of guys who'll do it."

"I'll take Lars and put him in bed at my tent," Curly said. "Did somebody get that laudanum?"

The excitement was wearing down. Preacher judged it to be about midnight or so, still a long night of work ahead.

The sheriff came and took charge of the bodies. He said that, "Yes, the Emporium did have a supply of coffins," and that he would handle it.

At last, Preacher headed up the trail to the school house. It seemed like he had left for the sheriff's office an eternity ago, but it had only been six or seven hours. It's just that so much had happened in those hours.

I forgot to tell the sheriff about the railroad, Preacher thought. *Oh well, tomorrow is soon enough.*

Chapter 37

The next day, a wagon rolled up to the school house, at 9:45am. Two men carried the caskets in and set them on benches in front of the slate board. A few minutes later, people began to arrive. Some of the women carried bunches of wildflowers they had gathered.

Finally, Lars and Curly arrived, looking like they had slept little, if at all.

The school house was filled to overflowing, and some people stood around the open door and windows looking in.

Preacher stood in front, holding his Bible.

At 10:00 the room hushed, and Preacher began to speak.

"We gather today, as lost, bewildered children, with many questions, and knowing little. We know that yesterday, the three lives represented here, were with us, and we enjoyed their presence in our lives. We are not alone in this situation. Many have been down this path before us, and each of us will exit this life at his or her appointed time, through the door marked death. None of us knows when that time will come for us. The Psalmist wrote that life is a vapor that is here briefly, and then is gone."

"What troubles us, is the manner of these deaths. We ask, why? Why so young, why at the peak of youth and vigor? Why so many at one time? Job had similar questions, I'm sure. His story is the oldest book in the Bible, and yet he had no more insight into the answers than we do. After he had lost all his sons and daughters at one time, he could do no less than we should do. In all faith and humility, Job said, 'The Lord giveth and the Lord taketh away. Blessed is the name of the Lord'. I stand here, today not having any fine, pious-sounding answers. But I know that the Lord loves us, cares for us, and has promised to take us to a better place. Dori and the children have gone to that better place ahead of the rest of us."

"In John's Gospel, chapter 14, Jesus told His disciples, 'Let not your hearts be troubled. You believe in God, believe also in Me. In My Father's house are many mansions. If it were not so I would have told you. I go to prepare a place for you, and if I go I will come again and receive you unto Myself that where I am, there you may be also. And where I go ye know, and the way ye know. Thomas saith unto Him, Lord we know not whither Thou goest, and how can we know the way? Jesus saith unto him, I am the Way, the Truth, and the Life no man cometh unto the Father but by Me'."

"I am reminded of a poem I once read that said in part, 'Safe in the arms of Jesus, safe on His gentle breast, finding as He promised, perfect peace and rest'." Please follow along to the graveside, and as we lay them to rest, know that what we are laying to rest is just their bodies, they are safe in the arms of Jesus."

Ten men stepped forward to carry the caskets out to the wagon, and then with Lars and Curly walking at the head of the procession, the mourners headed out to the freshly-dug graves.

Once there, Preacher said a prayer, the caskets were lowered into the earth, and Preacher picked up a handful of earth. "Dust to dust, ashes to ashes." he intoned, and dropped the earth into the graves. One by one, the mourners filed by the graves with those who had gathered wildflowers, dropping them into the open graves.

Then without further word, the mourners split up to go back home.

Chapter 38

Lars just disappeared. One moment he was there, and the next, he was gone. Curly swore that he had no idea where he had gone. He was just … gone.

A search was mounted because some thought that he might try to hurt himself in his grief, but there was no sign of him, and he was never seen by the town folks again.

"Well sheriff, what do you think happened to him?" The question was posed by Curly. "He was my friend, but he didn't say nothin' to me."

"I suspect he just couldn't face people around here, knowing that they knew what he'd done, and just took off to start over somewhere."

"It was an accident."

"Shore, but he couldn't take being reminded of it all the time, could you? At least that's my take on it."

"Makes me think of the story of Cain. Always roaming the earth, never finding rest," observed Preacher.

"Found out any more about any railroad, sheriff," asked Preacher.

"Nothin' yet."

"Well, with school winding down for the year, my contract with His'onor the Mayor is coming to a close. He said something last week about wanting me to stay on, but I've promised to be back in Haskell before summer. Hope his search for a headmaster is getting somewhere," Preacher mused.

"Knowing Hiz'onor like I do, he won't do anything until he knows he can't badger you into coming back next year."

"Well, I'm not 'badgering'. I have enjoyed the children, but he'd better get looking for a permanent solution. It's only fair to the children," Preacher said.

"You're preachin' to the choir," the sheriff laughed. "I just know the mayor."

"Well, come the end of May, I'm headin' back over the pass," Preacher said emphatically.

As the days grew warmer, Preacher's thoughts turned more and more to Haskell, and he felt the Lord was trying to tell him something.

Finally, with two weeks of the school year left, Preacher made a proposal to the students.

"You've all worked hard this year, and I think we have made real progress."

"Yeah, we can read lots better," said one of the twins.

"And I almost have my multiplication tables down perfect," said another boy.

"But I think the best thing is what we have learned about God," one of the younger girls said seriously.

"Well, I think it's about time we showed off a little," Preacher suggested. "You know, show your parents and friends that your time has not been wasted."

There was an explosion of excitement.

"Yeah... yeah. That would be great!"

"What I propose is to have an evening to invite your parents and friends. We'll have a spell-down, do some cipher exercises, and let each of you read, either from the reader, or… if you have something at home you want to read… as long as it's not too long. Then you can tell about the most important thing you learned this year."

"I'll have Sadie bake up some cakes, and she can bring coffee and punch. We'll have a party. How about it? You want to do it?"

"Wow, yes!" was the cry. The boys were jumping around with excitement, and the girls were already planning what dresses to wear.

"We'll invite Hiz'onor the Mayor, so he can see what the town's money bought. Oh, this will be fun," Preacher exclaimed. "Now, I want you on your best behavior, we're showing off. And of course, we'll want someone to explain our rules and how they came to be. Do I have a volunteer?"

All eyes turned to Tommy, but Johnny stood up and said, "I want to do it, Teacher."

"Are you sure, Johnny?"

"I'm sure, Teacher."

"All right, I know you'll do a good job!"

"Now, let's design and write out invitations for your parents and friends. I got some butcher paper from the Mercantile that we can draw our invitations on."

The students set to with a will, and soon the invitations were lettered and clutched in each hand to be delivered to their parents. Preacher had one to deliver to Hiz'onor personally.

"Now, the party has been set for the last day of school at 6:00 in the evening. Between now and then, we will practice our presentations, and get everything ready."

The students left for home in a festive mood.

Preacher walked down the hill to the Mayor's tent, to personally invite him to attend the party. Then he went to see Sadie and enlist her help.

Chapter 39

The campfire burned low... almost mere embers. Three men huddled around it, trying to catch the last of its warmth.

"I'm cold, d#@* it. Why can't we ever build up a fire big enough to get warm by?"

"'Cause we don't need someone coming to see what the fire is all about, that's why! 'Sides you're always cold. Why don't you just head to Mexico, and find a hot Senorita. That ought to warm you up. Haw, haw."

"I just might... How long are we going to stay out here, anyway? We ain't doin' no good. That old biddy is tough. She ain't never gonna sell out to you, Jake."

"I told you never to use my name, Toby. I'm Brother Eli, and if you slip at the wrong time, I'm goin' to shut that mouth of yours permanently."

"Yeah... yeah."

"You'll think 'yeah' when it happens."

"Look you two, this arguin' ain't getting us nowhere. But Toby's right boss, that old gal ain't so easy to drive off. We're wastin' time out here."

"When will you two ever learn to trust me? I'm way ahead of her. The answer should come any day now."

"You been saying that for a month now. 'Any day' sure is taking its time."

"When it gets here, you boys will wonder why you ever doubted me, and that ranch will just fall right into my hands."

"Just like that little dolly fell into your hands, back in Haskell?"

Eli's face turned a mottled red. "Why you...."

Toby backed hastily away. "I...I didn't mean to bump your sore paw, boss. But that one shore didn't work out like you planned."

Eli controlled himself with an effort, glaring at his offending companion. "That's another reason we stay here as long as it takes, he growled. "That mealy-mouthed preacher has got to be leaving West Fork any day. School is about done for the year, and he'll want to be on his way. He'll head over the pass to go see his other flock, and when he does, there won't be any help to get him out of trouble. I'll settle his hash once and for all."

Toby said nothing, but took a stick and stirred the dying embers.

"Guess I'll turn in, Ed offered. "Nothin' else to do."

"Yeah, you do that..."

Chapter 40

The day of the party dawned bright and clear. The children were antsy to get done and on to their summer break, but they were anxious to show off, too. So, their last practice went fairly smoothly, and they were in happy moods as they left the school house for home, to return later with their families.

Preacher set about cleaning up the school house for the last time.

Later in the afternoon, Sadie came up to the school house with little cakes she had baked for the occasion. She called them cookies, and said they were just little individual cakes she had baked up. She also brought cider and coffee. Preacher sampled one of the "cookies" and decided that maybe Sadie had something going for herself, and told her to serve them regularly, and her business might really boom.

Now they were ready, just waiting for guests.

About ten minutes later, the first families arrived and soon excited children were showing off "their" bench, "their" slate, "their" reader.

Preacher was everywhere, smiling, shaking hands, giving praise to the children. And soon it was time to begin their "show and tell." All who could find a seat, sat down, and the children, faces flushed with excitement and importance, began to show a typical day at school.

First, they had a spelling bee, which quickly came down to two of the girls, who battled it out to an eventual winner. The adults were impressed.

Then each child came up in front of the group, and read the passage they had selected. Parents, many of who could not read or write their own names, beamed as their child demonstrated their reading skill.

Finally, Preacher wrote some problems on the slate, and three students at a time went up and solved the problem, in front of the group. Once they had all solved their problem, they explained it to the group.

The parents loved it! They were so proud, that some of the women were even crying.

Then Johnny got up and explained about the school rules. How they were a small society, just as the town was a larger society, and how important the rules were to functioning and achieving their purpose of learning. Then he went on to tell how he had broken the rules, and the discipline that was administered, and how he had learned a lesson about God's grace through the process. He went on to say, "I'm not perfect, but I've sure changed a lot, since I gave my heart to Jesus."

The parents all knew about the rules and what had happened. But to hear and see Johnny's courage to tell about it, impressed them all.

Finally Preacher got up. "Well, that's all we have for you, tonight. Except, Sadie made us some little cakes she calls cookies. There is cider and coffee. Enjoy yourselves. Mr. Mayor, will you please end with a few words?"

A beaming mayor got to his feet. 'Isn't this something?" he asked. When I talked Preacher into doing this job, I had no idea that it would turn out so well. He's a born teacher, I tell you! It was money well-spent to get you to do this, Preacher. Let's show him how we feel about the job he's done."

With that, a great cheer went up, and people clapped and stomped until their hands were sore.

The Mayor interrupted the cheering to announce, "I'm going to try to get him back for next school year." Preacher just gave him a cold look.

"I'm not changing my mind, Mr. Mayor," he said.

"We'll see," answered Hiz'onor.

People headed for the refreshments, and everyone crowded around Preacher with congratulations and well-wishes.

"Yes, I'll be leaving for Haskell right away. I've been away from there longer than I had planned, and I know the people there are wondering if something happened to me," Preacher said in response to a question.

"Just so you're back in time for the next school year," the mayor called.

"I understand that you have a new man in town, a Mr. Thornberry, and that he is a former headmaster. Maybe, you'd better talk to him about next school year," Preacher suggested with a smile.

"Harrumph," said the mayor moving toward the refreshments.

The student began to come by, saying goodbye. "We'll miss you, Mr. Scott."

"Pete, remember what I talked to you about. You'll go a long way learning to control your temper. It's not easy, but God will help you if you ask Him."

Then, they were gone, and Preacher was alone. He felt a vague sense of loss. Well, tomorrow he'd be heading back to Haskell. He began to pick up the clutter.

Chapter 41

The next day was cloudy as Preacher saddled Noah, and slung his canteen, banjo, and possible sack over the saddle horn. He was just checking the cinch because Noah liked to blow up his stomach, especially when he had not been ridden for a while, when Hiz'onor rattled up in a buckboard.

"So, you're really gonna do it," he frowned.

"On my way," Preacher confirmed.

"But you will be back in time for school to start in September?"

"Don't count on me. You'd better talk to Mr. Thornberry. He's had experience and should be able to do a fine job," Preacher advised.

"You did a right fine job, and we want you to come back. Besides, your preaching took off. You have a real following, now."

Preacher smiled, thinking of the people who were now coming regularly to Sunday morning service. "You know, I *am* coming back to minister and see how they are doing, but I told Mr. Latimer and the others that I wouldn't be back until late October, or even into November. They can help keep the group together until I come back. I've got to check on the other people who expected me to come back in early spring. Being tied up in school wasn't part of the plan."

The mayor sighed. "Well, here is your final pay," and he tossed a small leather bag to Preacher. "You will be missed. Not just by me, either. Those children have never taken to a school master like they took to you. I think there is actually a chance for another head master to have success, now. If you do come back, I may even stop in to your 'church' to hear what you have to say. Not promising anything, mind you," he added hastily.

Preacher smiled. "You'd be welcome any time," he said. "Come on, Noah. We've got a ways to go." He climbed up into the saddle and pulled the mule around. "It was interesting," he called to the mayor, as he urged the mule down the trail toward the pass and out of town.

The mayor just sat there on the buckboard, watching until he went out of sight. Then he sighed again, picked up the reins and headed back into town.

CPSIA information can be obtained at www.ICGtesting.com
229336LV00002B/1/P